Bev Spicer v

1956. She attended the local grammar school and spent many a weekend learning to fly with her father at The Midland Gliding Club. After leaving school, she went on to study French and English Literature at Keele University, where she also became interested in astronomy, which she took as a subsidiary, and which led to a fascination with astrophysics and quantum theory. After taking up a secretarial post in London then working briefly as a croupier for Playboy, she decided to train to be a teacher. She graduated from Queens' College, Cambridge with a PGCE and completed her probationary year at Stantonbury Campus. She then left England to teach in Greece and later in Seychelles, before returning to Cambridge. Her most recent appointment was as lecturer in English as a Foreign Language, specialising in academic writing and English pronunciation at Anglia Ruskin University. She has held posts as an examiner for many Cambridge international examinations, including Regional Team Leader for the Cambridge Advanced Exam. She moved to France in 2008 with her husband and two youngest children, where she lives in a crumbly old house and writes full-time, when she is not stargazing.

Also by B. A. Spicer

Fiction

Hit and Run: a DCI Alice Candy case
An Incident at Brook House: a DCI Alice Candy case
My Grandfather's Eyes
Hit List
The Price of Love
What I Did Not Say

Non Fiction
by Bev Spicer

Memoir of an Overweight Schoolgirl
One Summer in France
Bunny on a Bike
Stranded in the Seychelles

LOCKED AWAY

B. A. SPICER

Cover design

by

SUE MICHNIEVICZ

Acknowledgements

I would like to thank Carrie-Ann Lahain, Karenne Griffin and Dylan Morgan for their generosity and expertise in helping to make Locked Away a better and more accomplished book. I would also like to thank Katie and Anna Philps for giving me invaluable early feedback on plot and characters. Sue Michniewicz has produced yet another stunning cover – what would I do without you, Sue! And my husband and family have continued to encourage me, even though this means I may have neglected them at times.

for Alice and Will

Chapter One

Ellie's body jerked and her eyes flicked open. Darkness. The sound that came from her mouth was muffled. Something approximating to *mah*! For a split second, she could not think. Then the questions came thick and fast: Where was she? Why was it so cold and dark? Why was she lying on the ground?

Her breathing quickened. Blinking, her mind still racing, she suddenly lay still and quiet, playing dead, trying to make sense of what was happening.

In the muddy darkness she couldn't see anything. No matter how widely she opened her eyes, there was no light. All around, it was deep dark like the dark of a forest at night, or a cave she'd visited as a child in Wales, where the lights had gone out before a lights show, leaving her thrilled and trembling. There would be no show here. That much was clear. She moved her shoulders and realised her hands were tied behind her back. It was an unlikely fact, but she took it in and once more her breaths came short and fast. Next, she registered pain: her arm hurt because she was lying awkwardly on it. She shifted again. Her nose flared and she smelled the dankness of stale earth beneath her, coarse against her skin, the individual pieces of grit and stone pressing into her.

The last thing she noticed was that she really was not able to speak because there was something covering her mouth. This was somehow much worse

1

than the darkness or the cord around her wrists. She tried again anyway but a stifled note, like a muted trumpet, was all that came out. Squeezing her tongue between her lips, she pushed and the tape pulled her skin but would not budge.

All these sensations became clear to her in seconds, almost but not quite simultaneously. Now she wore them like a new skin. A skin that made her feel vulnerable. Exposed.

Stay calm.

Not so easy, when what she felt inside was panic. A kind of panic that she'd never imagined she could feel. Thousands of sensors went off like fireworks in every organ of her body. At the same time, a terrible black silence flooded her head.

Where am I?

Ellie was not the kind of girl to get hysterical. It was time to take control. Steadying herself, she breathed in and out through her nose. Her pulse slowed. She lay still. There must be something to see in the darkness. The more she stared, the more she could make out. To her right, quite close by, there was a wall made of what looked like large stone blocks. She strained her eyes to see higher. Yes, there was the ceiling, not level, perhaps with beams. Beneath her, the floor was hard, uneven and darker than the wall. She felt once more its cold, grainy surface. Only then, did she register the fact that her bare skin was touching the earth. She was wearing a tee shirt and shorts. No shoes.

The strange air was cold against her body and, for a moment, Ellie was truly frightened. She knew also that she had never been really frightened before. Not even as a child. Not in the Welsh cave, or when she'd heard creaking on the stairs after her mother had gone to bed. Not when she'd stayed up late to watch a horror movie on her own. No, not ever. Here, where nothing made sense, she felt terror rising from her bowels. Wave after wave.

Come on, Ellie!

She gritted her teeth and banished the fear. Lying on her side, she had limited mobility. She sat up with difficulty, grazing the skin on her elbow and the side of her knee. When she was still again she listened to the sound of her own breathing, this time strategically, waiting for the quiet gaps to search the darkness for something other than the passage of air into and out of her lungs. And what if she did hear something?

Wriggling her toes, it was strange to imagine that her trainers and sports socks had been removed. Perhaps it was a precaution to make sure she couldn't run away... The outrage she felt was tempered by this petty preoccupation: Where were her shoes and socks? Ellie almost laughed. Then, the muscles in her abdomen tightened. Who the *hell* had done this to her? What right had *anyone* to do this to her!

It was time to focus, to assess the situation and do what she could. No point in dwelling on her plight. Action. She needed to act! First, she must free herself. The thin cord around her wrists hurt, and she made it hurt more when she twisted her hands to try to loosen it.

Think, Ellie!

It was made of something strong, like plastic. It was tight, but she had the feeling that it would stretch if she pulled at it enough. This thought gave her hope. This was good. Hope was essential in situations like this. In films, when victims were trapped, there was always a way out, no matter how dire the situation. The victims were actors, of course, and they knew that in the script there was an escape plan. She must find her own escape plan. If she were clever enough, there would be a way out.

As she worked on the cord she was able to pick out more detail in the darkness. To her right and further forward, set into the wall, there was the outline of something regular in shape. A door. Ellie held her breath and stared. Knowing there was a way out was a good thing, but knowing there was a way in...

Stop! Don't let it get to you!

Okay, so the door was there. Now that she'd seen it, she couldn't go back to the time before she'd noticed its fine, firm outline. So she would study it. To be ready, if it should open. It was not like an ordinary door. She remembered films she'd seen about prisons. The prison doors had a small window at the top that the guards could slide open so that they could look inside and check the prisoners were all right. This door had a window at the top with five small bars across it. Even if the bars had not been there, the window would surely not be big enough to fit her head through. If her head wouldn't go through, it would be pointless trying to fit the rest of her body into it. Pointless.

She continued her painstaking search. The worst thing was that nothing she saw made sense. Ellie had a hundred questions going round in her head and no one to answer them: Where am I? How did I get here? Why is it dark? Why are my hands tied?

But there was one question she didn't want to think about. One question that, nevertheless, kept coming back:

Is there anyone on the other side of the door?

Although this thought was ever present, it was important to continue with a logical and calm assessment of her situation. If there *was* a person on the other side of the door, that meant there was someone she could reason with. Everyone had a weak spot. Even people who were evil.

She knew there were evil people in the world. Men who killed women. Men who killed children. Even women who killed. There had been a man in Austria who had held a girl captive for years, until one day she had been rescued. Peter Sutcliffe - he had hated prostitutes enough to take them somewhere quiet in his car and strangle them. With her hands tied together, Ellie would not be able to stop a man strangling her. Even if she got a chance to bite him, to kick him, and even if by some miracle she then got the keys, how would she put the key into the lock? No! She shook her head to get such negative thoughts out of her mind and worked harder on the cord around her wrists. She grimaced against the pain, angry with herself for thinking about kidnappers and murderers and what they could do to her. With her hands free, she would feel better. Empowered. In the meantime, she should stick to positive thoughts.

The room was wide. She could not see much to the left or in front. Looking up, the ceiling seemed high and it appeared to be crossed with beams. There was a smell she recognised, too. What was it? It was damp and pungent, a bit like leaves in autumn when the rain falls on them and they turn soft on the street. But this smell was not as nice as wet leaves. Wet leaves made her think of being outside and looking up at the clouds in a big autumn sky. Here, there was no sky, there were no clouds, and the smell was old, like air that had not been changed for days or even weeks. It was not a healthy place to be and she tried not to breathe deeply, to keep the terrible air out of her lungs.

And suddenly it came to her. It must be a cellar. Of course! That meant there was a house above and someone who lived in it. A house with carpets and soft furnishings, electric light and central heating, windows and a view onto a street. Unless the house was in the middle of nowhere. In a forest or on a cliff top with the wind buffeting against it and the sea crashing below. It might be stormy outside. It might be sunny. It might be night. No matter what it was like, it would be better than where she was.

Just then, there was a tickle under her thigh and she was distracted by another scary thought: perhaps there were insects on the floor or on the walls. Maybe big spiders hanging from the ceiling, perhaps just above her head, waiting to fall on her. The thought made her squeak, like a frightened animal. A small squeak, like a mouse. The sound of her voice was strange inside the room and the silence after it stranger. The memory of it echoed inside her head, until she thought: *How can I be afraid of spiders, when my hands are tied and I don't know where I am?? How can I be so stupid?*

Working harder at the cord, Ellie planned ahead: *What shall I do when my hands are free? When I get the tape off my mouth should I shout for help, or should I stay quiet?* These were important, practical considerations. It would be key to her survival that she chose the right option.

Just then, outside the door, she heard a sound. It was the sound of a muffled cough. And she froze. It proved that someone was there listening and, what a horrible thought, *watching*.

Chapter Two

Dom got off the bus and walked through the park into town, squinting in the sunshine and wishing he'd remembered his sunglasses. The lines across his forehead made him look older than he was. The stubble he wore gave him a rough and ready look, he knew, in contrast to his long, blond hair.

He pushed up his shirt sleeves and adjusted his watch strap, which was new and too tight. Two young women passed close to him and smiled. He turned to look, wondering if he knew them. They looked back at the same time and one of them giggled. Dom shook his head. He was unconvinced by his alleged power over women. But as his friends said, *There's no accounting for taste. If they want to look, let them!* When Dom smiled to himself, two small lines appeared either side of his mouth. A tall girl with long dark hair almost stopped. *You have a killer smile, you know?* Ellie had told him once.

Dom looked straight ahead, making out detail in the distant views of the river, the tall trees that bordered it, remembering a punting trip that had gone badly wrong, which made his smile even wider.

He quickened his pace. It was a relief to be out of the classroom. Sometimes, cooped up in school all day he almost regretted the change he had made in his career, but mostly he knew that working in an office had been much, much worse. He would do a good job as a Maths teacher when he qualified. Until then it would be tough.

At twenty-six, he was still young compared with most of the other teachers. And he was better equipped than the probationers just out of university, to deal with the difficult kids.

I don't get it, sir. I've never been any good with numbers. Rosaline Warner always stayed after class to ask him something. Anything. Today, she had unbuttoned her blouse and leaned in with an unnerving teenage leer. *I like your hair, sir. Don't cut it, will you?* She smelled of soap and chewing gum, and wore a vacant expression.

Then there was Rosaline's much prettier friend, Christine. *Leave him alone, Rosa. He's not interested.* Christine Riley spoke with a permanent sneer and moved with a habitual swagger.

Dom could handle the attention, the schoolgirl crushes. The secret was not to take it seriously, not to let it get to you. He smiled again, shaking his head, as was his habit. Who cared? Right now, he was out! Away from it all. He'd been for a swim and his body buzzed. He ran a hand through his still damp curly hair and thought of Ellie.

It was Friday. At last the weekend had arrived – it was great to have some free time ahead of him. The kids had been just as excited as he was to escape the confines of the school building. Full of life, derisive and fickle, they'd barrelled out of the gates and lingered in untidy groups, smoking, laughing and cursing. *Bye, sir. See you on Monday, sir. Thanks for the lesson on fractions, sir.* There was something so right about their absolute disdain of authority.

With images of the day running through his mind and still feeling the pleasant after effects of the time he'd spent in the pool, he made his way through the busy shopping mall and outside again to an area where independent shopkeepers had taken over a network of small streets, ending in a cul-de-sac. The narrow pavements were strewn with potted plants so people were forced to step out into the road – there were rarely any cars, just the odd delivery van. There were colourful signs and a bustling café. Tucked away between this and a shop selling herbal remedies, there was a tiny jeweller's workshop with a minuscule window display and a narrow red door that stood perpetually open.

When he entered, the woman glanced up and smiled.

"I thought you'd be back," she said, laying aside her tools with gentle grace.

"You know me too well," replied Dom. It was not the first time he'd made a purchase.

She nodded and stood up from her chair, looking outside as though surprised to see so many people gathered drinking coffee at the tables. "Is that the time already?"

Dom watched her move slowly towards a tall cupboard that housed a number of pieces reserved for customers. He wondered how many years this woman had spent sitting in her tiny workshop manipulating precious metals and rare stones with the help of a bright spotlight and a large magnifying glass. The tools she used were laid out like surgical instruments on a clean moleskin cloth.

She returned with a box and set it down on the counter. "Would you like to look again?"

Dom lifted the lid and took out a silver necklace, the heart shaped pendant rounded at the top and flattened at the bottom so that it looked as though it had been squeezed. About the size of a pound coin, it was simple, yet original. It was exquisite.

"I think the finer chain is best," said the shopkeeper, cocking her head to one side.

Dom ran his fingers along it. It was almost invisible. He put the necklace back in the box. "Thank you, I'll take it. It's perfect."

Outside, he bought a coffee and sat at one of the tables. Ellie would be home. She'd got the afternoon off. She'd probably be stretched out, taking a long bath. Perhaps he should call round earlier than arranged. The restaurant was booked for seven thirty – there was time. The thought made his whole face smile.

Dom sipped his coffee and watched the ordinary-looking people going in and out of the unusual shops. It was almost five o'clock. The coffee tasted good. He sat back and thought about Ellie up to her lovely neck in bubbles. Ellie was just twenty-one, fun, intelligent and beautiful. He was a lucky man.

Chapter Three

Still working on the cord, Ellie listened with every part of her body. She felt as though electricity were running through her, sensitising her skin, feeding her pulse – this must be how an animal felt when it was being hunted. Stunned by expectation. Preyed upon. She gritted her teeth – anger, not fear rose in her chest.

She was sure there was still someone on the other side of the door, and equally sure that he was observing her. She forced herself to think about it logically: If he could see her, then she should be able to see him without moving position. Yes. That was the way it worked. But there was a shutter behind the bars in the small window that remained closed. There was no other obvious place he could be using. Unless he was looking through a small hole in the door! This new idea made her shiver, because she felt as though it must be true.

She resisted the urge to shout out. What good would it do? Especially as the tape was still securely fixed over her mouth. No, she would hold firm. It was imperative that she get control of the situation – if she was being watched, she must not show any weakness and so, putting her head down for a moment, Ellie closed her eyes and tried to think of something else. Something normal. Her wrists were sore, but the tie was weakening.

The first thing that came into her mind was Dom's

face. He was smiling at her and telling her he would see her later. The thought made a lump rise in her throat and, just for a second, tears threatened to come. But she focused once more, squeezing her eyes tight shut. Dom. He would come to her house at seven o'clock to take her out to a restaurant for her birthday. Her birthday! No. Don't get distracted. Think!

Dom would knock on the door and there would be no answer. She imagined him standing there, looking confused and knocking again, harder this time. He would look at his watch and wonder where she was. Then he would call her on her mobile.

Where's my phone? The person on the other side of the door might have it!

Somehow this new realisation was even more of a violation than being locked away in a cellar. He had her phone! If he managed to unlock it he could look at the photographs of her friends and family, and of her. The screen saver was a picture of Dom kissing her. It made her feel sick to think of the person who was outside the door looking at them kissing. It made her feel sick and indignant, too. How dare he! She shook her head from side to side and felt a furious heat rising in her cheeks. If he were there, watching her, she would let him know that she *knew* he was there. That she despised him and was not afraid.

With new determination, she searched the door for a hole, a gap. It was still difficult to see much in the darkness, but the door was a lighter colour than the walls. Perhaps it was painted. And then she saw it. Next to the small window. A hole. Big enough for a person to look through. She stared at it, with wide, angry eyes. Her body shook, but not because she was afraid.

Then, she heard a different sound. Like a person laughing softly, walking away and laughing. And she realised with a new wave of frustration that perhaps the man had waited for her to find the hole. He had wanted her to know that he was watching her, just as she had wanted him to know that she was not afraid. He was playing a game. And then, for the first time, it occurred to Ellie that he might be crazy. That would make things more difficult. She remembered the laugh and tried to imagine what he was like. Was he old or young? Was he strong or weak? Was he going to hurt her? Or was he going to keep her here just to look at?

Left alone once more, Ellie worked more determinedly on the cord that bound her wrists. And, as she worked, grimacing at the cutting pain, she tried to remember what had happened to her. To understand how she'd arrived in this place.

Come on, Ellie! Come on! You have to remember!

Gradually, although her thoughts were muddled, she began to recall a few details: She was inside her house. There was her room, the bedside table, with the photograph of Dom standing on the beach in Brighton. The merry-go-round a colourful blur behind him. His miraculous smile. The black blinds at her window were open. Blue sky. Yes. That was it. She'd gone up to her room to change her shoes – to put on her trainers. What then? Back downstairs, gliding a hand along the banister, making a face in the mirror and opening the front door. It was odd how clearly the images came to her now. Outside, she'd waved to Mr. Edwards on the other side of the street and taken the main road, cutting through the allotments towards the local shops. That was it! She'd gone to the Co-op to get milk and bread. She'd spoken to Mrs. Adams and said that it was her birthday. Mrs. Adams had been surprised because her daughter's birthday was on the same day. Then what? She thought hard but it made her head hurt. It was difficult to keep the continuity of what had happened.

For a moment, she was aware of the cold ground beneath her and the darkness all around. Her body felt weak and aching, too. Had he drugged her? Why couldn't she think straight? She shivered again. It was the middle of summer outside, but down here in this small room made of stone and earth, it was cold. And as silent as the grave.

Having lost the thread of her recollections, her thoughts came back to the cellar room. She could see better now, and she scanned the shadowy corners once again to see what more would be revealed. There was something over on the left and further back. She stood up carefully, not trusting her legs, not wanting to lose her balance and fall over. Her hands were still tied and she found it hard to balance. She went forward slowly, putting her bare feet down tentatively, gripping the earth with her toes.

Could it be? The thought was comforting and yet, at the same time, chilling. Yes! It was a bed. A bed! And there, at one end, was a pillow and a blanket. Ellie wrenched at the cord around her wrists again and this time she felt it give a little more so that she was able to wriggle her hands until, at last, she felt a slackness and the cord slipped onto the ground behind her. Ellie rubbed her wrists, but in spite of the soreness, she felt good.

Pulling off the tape that covered her mouth and throwing it to the ground, she sat down on the thin mattress and put the blanket around her shoulders to keep herself warm. It was soft. It smelled of fabric conditioner. Someone had provided clean bedding, as though they were expecting her to need it. Another thought struck her: *Had all this been planned?* And yet another: *Had it been planned for a random victim, or just for her?*

The latter thought added a new layer of discomfort and menace.

How did I get here? What is this place?

Ellie closed her eyes and pulled the blanket more tightly around her. Where had she been? Mrs. Adams' shop. Yes. She had bought bread and milk at the corner shop – the sign had been newly painted and the door, too. The smell of paint. There'd been a piece of paper flapping, saying 'WET PAINT' in big, handwritten capital letters.

Detail came easily. Too much detail. She had waited at the counter with her purchases. The counter stained by greasy fingers, the occasional spillage and scratches from years of use. Mrs. Adams was busy organising an afternoon delivery of magazines. The back of her skirt swung from side to side as she bent over bundles, unwrapping them. She had spoken without looking round: *I haven't had time to get these out. I won't be a minute.* Ellie had said she was in no hurry. She'd been hungry and her stomach had growled loudly. She was going to make a sandwich. Just a small one, because in the evening she was going out with Dom.

Dom. Would he know she was missing yet? Concentrate. Get back to the shop!

Mrs. Adams was talking about deliveries. Saying they never arrived when you wanted them to. Her shoulders moved as she worked to untie the bundles. Her skirt swayed more. She knew that Ellie was waiting.

Then what? Try to remember, Ellie.

In the end, Mrs. Adams had stood up straight, turned, and with a crooked, slightly embarrassed smile had asked Ellie how she was. That was when Ellie had told her it was her birthday. The conversation played itself out in her mind, word for word, when all she wanted was to remember what happened next. Why were her thoughts so slow and meticulous?

She breathed deeply and the smell of fabric conditioner was almost overpowering, bringing her back to the present.

No, shut it out. Remember!

More irrelevant detail came back to her until eventually she saw herself coming out of the shop carrying a thin plastic carrier bag. Ellie could feel the weight of the milk and bread making the handles push into the folds of her fingers. Outside, in the bright sunshine, she had followed the road and taken the narrow path that went past the allotments. A short cut. Everywhere was green, so green. With flowers. So many flowers. Never had colours seemed so vibrant!

There was no one in the vegetable gardens. It was strangely quiet in the dull heat of the afternoon. She'd walked past the huge oak tree with its spreading branches, and then? There'd been a bench. She'd sat down. Yes. She'd sat down and opened her can of Sprite. Yes, she'd bought a drink in the shop, too. Strange that she hadn't remembered this before. Must have been an afterthought.

What else have I forgotten?

She'd taken the first sip – cold, sweet, with bubbles that burst on her tongue. She could feel the wooden bench beneath her and smell the synthetic lemon from the can. And when she'd tilted her head to take a second and third gulp, someone had spoken. Behind her. Someone had whispered her name! The shock of remembering made her gasp.

Hello, Ellie!

She didn't have time to turn around. After remembering someone say her name, hearing the urgent whisper, not knowing who had voiced it, she couldn't seem to get any further. It was as if her life had stopped at that moment. Until the time she had woken up in this small dark room. If only she could be back at the corner shop, where there were people she knew. If only she could feel the carrier bag swinging beside her.

No! It will be all right. You are stronger than this!!

Ellie felt the warmth of the blanket. Then she

noticed the low table with a water bottle and a plastic glass. Next to it was a bucket with a lid on it. When she lifted the lid, there was a strong smell of chemicals. A thought slipped through her mind, *Everything a person needed to stay alive. Apart from food.* Then she knew there was a way forward – he would bring food. He would open the door and provide her with something to eat. Otherwise none of the other things made sense.

Yes. He has put these things here for me. He has planned all of this. There is a bed, a blanket, water, a makeshift toilet. He is going to keep me here for a long time, perhaps forever. I am locked away and no one knows where I am. It's up to me to find a way out of this. It's up to me!

Ellie had an empty feeling in her stomach. At first she thought that it might be hunger but she realised that it was a much stronger feeling than that. It was a surge of adrenalin, a tensing of muscles. She was going into battle with her captor. And she was going to win.

She stared into the darkness and imagined the door opening. She would be ready when it did.

Chapter Four

At home, Dom showered. There were pink tiles and blue fish swimming anti-clockwise, disappearing behind a silver shower curtain. He wished he had his own place. Living at home allowed him to save on rent. But living at home sucked.

He pulled on his black jeans and a tee shirt Ellie liked. Then he went back to the bathroom and cleaned his teeth, staring into the mirror once more, wondering whether his nose was crooked and his eyebrows too thick. *You worry too much!*

Grabbing his shoes and slipping on a wristband he liked to wear, he picked up the present – beautifully wrapped and with a plain card attached – and went downstairs. He was hungry and the smell of dinner coming from the kitchen made him hungrier.

"You look good!" said his mother when he came into the kitchen.

"Thanks. What's on the menu tonight?"

She hadn't finished – put her nose to his neck. "Good enough to eat!"

"Okay, that's a bit weird," said Dom's younger brother, Eddie.

Dom laughed. It was a bit weird, and Eddie knew that he knew it was.

"Don't be so daft. I'm allowed to pay your brother a compliment, surely? You're probably going to grow up to be twice as handsome, anyway!" She ruffled Eddie's short brown hair.

"Mum!" Eddie stood up, then sat down again, going back to his texting with a frown.

"How's it going, Ed?" Dom pulled out a chair and sat opposite.

"School's boring. Home's boring. Life's boring." His phone made a sound and he looked back to the screen.

"That bad, eh?" Dom winked at his mother, who was stirring a pot of something on the stove.

Eddie scowl grew and he groaned. "And my brother's going to be a teacher! A boring old maths teacher."

"Yep. Don't know how *that* happened." Dom grinned. He remembered only too well what it was like to be sixteen. "Fancy a quick thrashing before dinner?"

Eddie looked up from his phone with a little more interest. "Thought you were going out?"

"I am. But there's time, if you're up for it."

When Dom came downstairs again his mother hugged him and said, "Thanks. He needed that."

"He's a great kid. He'll be fine, don't worry."

His mother sighed. Eddie was hard work. She looked at Dom and spoke more quietly. "Ellie's a lucky girl. I remember when your father looked as good as you do. All those years ago."

"Hey! What do you mean?" said his father, who was sitting in front of the television.

"Only joking," said his mother, grinning at her son.

"Don't think I can't *see* you!" said his father, laughing.

"Well, your eyesight *is* getting worse," she replied, laughing back.

"Luckily for you!"

His mother didn't like that quite as much.

"What time are you meeting Ellie?" she asked.

"I'm picking her up at around seven." Dom watched his mother move around the kitchen. She was always busy doing something.

"Are you going to *Fernando's*?"

"It's *Nando's*, Mum," said Dom, smiling.

"Oh, well, you know what I mean!"

"Lucky someone does!" said a voice from the sitting room.

Dom looked at his watch and picked up his keys from the sideboard. "I'd better get going. Bye, Dad, see you later!"

"Bye, son. Behave yourself! Don't do anything *I* wouldn't do!"

It was what his father always said.

"Have a good time," said his mother, rolling her eyes, "and don't drink too much."

"Don't worry, Mum," he said, kissing her cheek. "You worry too much, you know?"

Living at home for a while had its advantages, but the sooner Dom could leave, the better. Moving out, though, was definitely not an option at the moment. Not until he qualified and got a permanent teaching job. The money he'd saved from his previous job would make a healthy deposit on a house, but he needed to be able to meet the monthly payments as well. Until then he would have to put up with the constant care and attention, the intrusive questions and petty house rules.

Eddie had asked him more than once how long he was going to stay – a desperate look on his face. There was no disguising the fact that he liked having his older brother around.

When Dom had worked away, visits home had been infrequent and he knew that Eddie relished the extra time they could spend together now. This time, when he moved out, Dom would make sure it was not so far away.

Outside, it was still a nice evening. Warm enough to sit outside at Nando's and have a cocktail before their meal.

Ellie loved cocktails. She loved to eat out. It was difficult to find anything Ellie didn't like – she had enthusiasm in huge amounts, always putting a positive slant on even the most unpromising situations. He was hooked. These simple thoughts made him feel excited and scared at the same time. Getting down on one knee was the next logical step. It would happen, but not tonight. Tonight, it was Ellie's birthday and he had the present he'd chosen for her in his pocket. It was going to be a great evening.

He drove to Harrington Avenue and parked outside number eleven. Ellie lived alone, in her parents' house. They'd bought a villa in Spain and had given the house to Ellie to look after while they were away. It was in a good area and the large, detached houses were worth a lot of money. Ellie's family were much better off than Dom's. But that didn't matter. Ellie said that money wasn't important. Dom didn't know whether he agreed about that. A teacher's salary wouldn't keep them both, that was for sure. But when Ellie qualified as a nurse, they would manage well enough.

As he walked up the steps to the front door, Dom noticed that there were no lights on at the front of the house. Ellie must be in the lounge or the study, at the back. She normally left the light on in the hall, though, even in summer. He knocked, examining the knocker, which had come from France. It was in the shape of a hand. The Braintrees had style, that was certain.

Ellie didn't come. There was no sound of footsteps running down the hall, no turning of the latch. Dom knocked again, more loudly. Then he looked at his watch: seven o'clock. He waited. A car passed by and a child shouted across the street to his friend. Dom tried a third time, but it was obvious by now that there was no one in the house. He turned and looked up and down the street. Where could she be? There was no one to ask, apart from the two children who were now running in the opposite direction. He could call at one of the neighbours' houses. But what would he say? He knocked one last time, with no expectation of anyone coming to the door. No answer.

Dom took his mobile phone out of his pocket and selected Ellie's number. He listened to it ring and go to answer phone.

"Hi Ellie. It's Dom. Where are you? I'm outside your house. Give me a call when you get this message and I'll come and get you." He hesitated, not knowing how to finish the message. Then he said, 'Happy birthday, Ellie.'

Chapter Five

Missing persons. Case number thirty-five. Ellie Braintree. Twenty-one years old, shoulder-length blond hair, blue eyes, chicken pox scar above her left eyebrow, one metre sixty-three, forty-eight kilos, medium build.

The photo was recent. Taken from her Facebook page, which was presently a hotbed of messaging. Friends asking questions, well wishers. The usual comments. Heartfelt. It was a comfort to the parents. But it was leading precisely nowhere. In fact people could be too helpful and end up wasting police time. And time was invariably the deciding factor in this kind of investigation. In her experience, Inspector Alice Candy knew that if a missing person wasn't found in the first forty-eight hours then the odds were that they would not be found at all, and if they were, it would almost certainly not be alive. Despite all this, Alice Candy's gut instinct told her that Ellie was alive. Alive and well. Gut instinct was always more reliable than statistics.

The morning had been just like any other. Alice Candy had arrived at eight-thirty, called a meeting at nine, and begun routine work at her desk at ten. She'd had no clue that anything was amiss. Although, now she thought about it, there had been something. Not much, but something. Before leaving the house, she always left food out for Cleo. On this particular morning, she'd had to fetch spare supplies from the cupboard under the stairs. Cleo had accompanied her, nudging her ankles and purring. The light switch hadn't worked at first. She'd pushed it several times and in the end the bulb had flickered and come on. Inside the enclosed space there'd been a strange smell. Dank and heavy. At the time, she'd put it down to damp, but there was no damp in the house. Never had been. When she'd looked round, Cleo had disappeared. Normally, the cat would pad behind her and wait for Alice to take the box down from the shelf. Perhaps there were other things she'd missed. It had been a long time since her intuition had come into play. She might be getting rusty.

There was something else. Now it came to her. When Will Brady, looking too good to be true, had come into her office with a tell-tale frown on his face, the second thought Alice Candy had had was of a door closing. A heavy door, with a latch and a key that turned in its lock. Her first thought had had nothing to do with Ellie Braintree.

Will had handed her a folder and sat down heavily. He'd left her twenty minutes later to follow up a couple of lines of enquiry.

All this had happened on Monday morning.

The facts of the case lay on the desk before the inspector now: Ellie Braintree had disappeared two days ago. Last seen walking along Chey High Street, away from the convenience store run by a Mrs. Adams, who remembered Ellie saying it was her birthday, and who had told the police that Ellie had seemed perfectly happy. The girl had purchased bread, milk and a soft drink, and had left the shop at around four-thirty in the afternoon.

Alice Candy stopped reading to examine a broken nail. It would have to be just before her daughter's wedding day! Would there be time for it to grow back? She'd got the perfect shade of varnish to go with the pink dress she'd bought. Now her nails would look odd. Perhaps she could get a false, stick-on nail. Maybe that would work.

Will Brady stuck his head round her door. "Just off home, Boss – unless you need me for anything?" His eyebrows shot up.

Alice swallowed hard. "No, you get off. Nothing happening that I can't deal with. In fact nothing much happening at all."

Will looked down at his feet and then back to the inspector. "Right. See you in the morning, then."

"No doubt." She did not return his smile.

The door closed and Alice Candy watched her colleague through the glazed partition as he returned to his desk. Will was an enthusiastic and hard-working officer. He had bags of energy and a good brain. The fact that he had film star looks was beside the point. Late twenties, single and handsome – the women in the office enjoyed having him around. Shifting in her chair and silently reprimanding herself, Alice returned to Ellie Braintree's file. There had to be something. If only she could find it.

The inspector was a woman of unusual style. Tall and slim, with good legs, she wore her dark hair short, cut into the nape of her neck and swept to one side at the front. She had a habit of twisting any stray curls that fell forward around her left ear when she was concentrating. People said she had magnificent eyebrows. They were arched, giving her an air of being permanently surprised. She knew that her eyes were small, but they were of the darkest brown and bordered by beautifully long eyelashes. She wore little makeup, but liked a dab of lipstick. She didn't favour trousers. She wore dresses rarely. At work, she preferred a skirt and blouse, occasionally accompanied by a fitted jacket. Only needing a low heel, Alice Candy chose expensive shoes, and enjoyed the comfort and elegance of sheer stocking holdups. At home, she wore exquisitely made fitted kaftans and embroidered slippers.

A curl fell forward and she wound it around her finger, pushing it back.

Two hours later, the telephone rang.

"Mum?"

Inspector Candy blinked, looking out of her office window onto deserted desks and extinguished strip lights. Her daughter's voice pulled her into a different, lighter world. "Jude?"

"Do you know what time it is?"

Doubtless, it was the wrong time. Doubtless she had overlooked something important. "Was I supposed to be doing something today?"

"Mum! We were going to meet at the florist's at six o'clock. You know, to make the final selections."

Alice Candy groaned.

Her daughter spoke kindly. "It's all right. Rachel came with me. I think it's sorted."

"Sorry, Jude. It's just…"

"I know. Ellie Braintree. Don't apologise, Mum. I know she needs you even more than I do."

It wasn't what Alice was thinking at all. She was thinking that she was a terrible mother, that her daughter was knee-deep in wedding plans and had wanted her to be part of it all. Just in a small way. Flowers. She had wanted her mother to meet her at the florist's. That was all. Hopeless. Unforgivable.

But Jude was right about one thing – Ellie Braintree did need her. Ellie was the same age as

Jude. Just a girl. And Ellie's mother? She would not be choosing roses or wondering about which bouquets were most appropriate. The poor woman would be falling apart and, even with hope running out, she would be holding on to the thought that it was never too late. Never too late for her daughter to be returned to her. Alice Candy felt the weight of her hope. And she again had the strongest premonition that, this time, the girl could be found. In her mind's eye, she pictured Ellie, shrouded in darkness. It was a strong intuition. She would work on it. Looking for a pathway. Just as she had done each night so far.

"Are you still there, Mum? Are you okay?"

The image that was forming in her mind dissipated. "Jude? Yes. Yes, I'm all right. Just a bit tired. Can we…"

"Sure. Let's leave dinner tonight. Hugo and I are done in, as well. Shall I see you next Monday afternoon? You remember we've booked a hairdresser and manicurist for a trial run?"

Alice Candy scribbled the details on a scrap of paper and said, "Got it. That'll be perfect. Sorry, darling."

"No need to be. Just get some rest now, Mum. And good luck. If anyone can find Ellie, you can."

Locking the door to her office and making her way down to reception, where the night shift officers were settling in, Alice hoped that her daughter's faith in her was not misplaced. There were eleven clear days before Jude and Hugo's wedding. More than anything, Alice Candy wanted to be there in the knowledge that she had done all she could for the Braintree family.

When she got home, Cleo was waiting for her in the kitchen.

"I know what you want. I'm late. I know. Do you forgive me?"

Cleo wound herself around Alice's legs and waited patiently for her to open a packet and tip its contents into a saucer.

"There. Now let me think. I have to think." She stooped to stroke the cat and felt its skin ripple beneath a thick layer of fur.

Alice Candy heated a ready meal and ate it standing up at the kitchen work-surface. With a quiet mind, she pictured Ellie Braintree, first in the pictures she remembered from Facebook, then at the corner shop, then walking home, swinging a flimsy carrier bag. The carrier bag had come to her most recently. It was semi-transparent and tinted blue.

She cleared the sideboard and opened a drawer, taking out a new candle and pushing it into a pewter holder. When it was lit, she placed it on the table and extinguished the lights. The kitchen, with its bare floor and sparse furniture seemed more appropriate, less cluttered than the other rooms in the house. It was where she had meditated (this was how Alice preferred to think of her 'gift') since Ellie had been reported missing. It was where images had begun to form of a girl shut away, alone and in relative darkness. And, going deeper, sensing a certain energy, she had come to believe that this girl was alive. That she was strong. That she would fight and perhaps survive.

Cleo jumped up onto her mistress' lap and began to purr.

Alice Candy stroked her soft fur in the darkness and remained silent and still, her eyes wide open and her thoughts travelling to who knew where.

Chapter Six

It was difficult to judge the passing of time in the cellar room. There was just a gradual and barely noticeable ebb and flow of shadows. In the silence, the grey settled and condensed like vapour, stirred by a narrow strip of weak daylight that came in through a ventilation gap at the top of the outside wall, which must be at ground level. The thought of being so close to the outside world and of the possibility of somehow scaling the wall to work at the opening had occupied Ellie for almost two days. But, in the end, when she'd tried turning the bed on end and using it as a ladder, standing on tip-toe, searching for footholds in the wall and still finding herself half a metre away from the slender exit, she'd given up. She had no tools, anyway. And the gap was too narrow by far.

Now, in a place so very cut off, she began to feel safe, in a strange way. Her mind trimmed down to basics. She owned the space. She would survive. And, in the end, she would prevail over her enemy, who deserved nothing from her but contempt.

Ellie knew roughly how long she'd been locked away by the welcome arrival of feeble daylight and the inevitable falling of the lonely night. She'd also counted the meals she'd been brought - etching marks in the corner, on the bare ground. She was pretty sure she was fed three times a day. Keeping a record was important. It gave her a sense of order.

When the door had clicked open for the first time, she'd been asleep. By the time she'd sat up, whoever had pushed the tray inside had gone again, as quietly as a ghost. She'd shouted, without stopping to think.

"Hello! Who's there? Open the door! Wait!"

She'd leapt up, banged on the door and pressed her face to the peep hole, her blinking eyelashes catching its edges, her heart pounding. Grabbing at barely perceived images, there had been a dimly lit passageway, then there had been darkness again. And silence. That was the first time Ellie had really cried. Whether it had been from fear or frustration, she couldn't have said. Her throat had constricted and the tears had come in huge droplets. Almost as soon as the outburst of emotion had arrived, it had subsided, leaving a hard core of something like determination in the centre of her chest. She'd eaten the bread and soup, saving the chocolate bar and the apple. She'd taken off the clothes she'd been wearing and put on the clean dressing gown and slippers that arrived in a plastic bag. Calmly and logically, she began to work on her abductor's profile.

If he'd wanted me dead he would have killed me by now.

On subsequent visits, she noted that he always came when she was lying down on the bed. Even if she wasn't asleep, he was too quick for her to catch him. And he never spoke. For the first two days, she'd called after him aggressively, pleadingly, delivering no particular message other than the fact that she wanted to be released. Soon, though, she took a different tack.

"I need a lamp. And something to read. I want my

clothes."

Next time, there'd been a small torch and three paperbacks.

"Thank you," she'd said.

Soon, she'd accumulated two pens, a writing pad, crayons and drawing paper. She'd received a towel and clean clothing – jogging bottoms, a tee shirt and a zip-up jacket. There was a tiny sink in the farthest corner she'd not noticed at first, with soap, toothpaste and a toothbrush. On the first day, she'd tipped away the contents of the bucket, but the smell had been unbearable without new chemicals and so she had left the bucket by the door. He had cleaned it and brought it back replenished.

"I'd like some matting. The earth is dirty. I like to be clean."

He'd pushed in a small roll of carpet.

"I'd like some deodorant."

He'd delivered a gift box of perfume and body spray.

"I need light. Real daylight I don't want to be in darkness."

This had not been granted.

Although he never spoke, Ellie knew that he listened to her. He paid attention to her words and the emotions that they conveyed. She could not see him through the peep hole, but, after the door had closed, she sensed that he waited. Waited to make sure she was all right. And in the silence, Ellie believed that he wanted to make everything good. It was a strange and conflicting sensation. He would not speak, he would not open the door, but he wanted to make her comfortable. Even to make her happy. What kind of person would try to do that? What kind of person would not understand that she would never submit to being a prisoner?

Despite the concessions he had made, with the next delivery of food, Ellie lost patience. She'd been thinking about Dom, her mother and father, her friends. They'd be going through hell.

"You need to let my family know I'm all right. Please. It's important to me."

On the tray, she'd left a note with two telephone numbers clearly written.

The note had come back with no comment, no clue. She'd tried again, speaking from the heart, making her voice soft and just a little vulnerable. Maybe he wanted to know that he had power over her. Nothing.

Ellie worked out a routine: sleep, wash, exercise, eat, read, draw, write. She tried not to think too much about the outside world. If she did, her mind just went in circles. It was better to concentrate on practicalities: stay fit and healthy, be ready to act decisively if the opportunity arose.

One question, however, burned and refused to be extinguished. It led nowhere. It left her feeling weak. She could not imagine what the answer might be.

What did he want with her?

Sometimes, she thought that, no matter what it was, she would like to know.

Chapter Seven

It was early evening and Dom sat in the kitchen, his thoughts wandering, the evening stretching out before him. He had no plan.

His early morning and after school swims had been replaced at first by helping the police in their search for Ellie.

Dom had covered every inch of the town and been out with the police and members of the public in the surrounding countryside for hours on end. He'd walked the route from the corner shop to Ellie's house with her parents, her friends, and on his own, at all times of the day and night. Everyone he'd met, he'd shown the picture of Ellie he kept in his wallet. No one had seen her. But they'd all seen the posters around the town: 'Have you seen this girl?' Most of them already had a look in their eyes when he pulled out the photo. They were looking at a dead girl. That's what the look said.

At school, he couldn't concentrate. His lesson plans and marking lay on his desk unfinished. The Head sent him home in the end. "Take some time. Come back when you feel able."

Dom hadn't argued. He was too exhausted to argue. He didn't eat and he didn't sleep. But he did smoke. As soon as one cigarette was finished, he lit another. His parents had said nothing. He knew that they hated seeing him like this. He'd stopped swimming completely now, stopped working too, just sat at home thinking, watching the news in his room, waiting for something, anything to happen.

Twice a day, he contacted Alice Candy and her team. Twice a day, he was told that there was no news on Ellie's case. *No news is good news*, his father told him, but anyone could see that his heart wasn't in it. He just wanted to comfort his son.

The worst thing was that after the initial flurry of activity, there was little to do. Dom felt useless. Ellie had disappeared and he could do nothing about it. He'd tried everything. The best hope had been Ellie's phone. The police had confirmed that it had been switched off. Was it lost somewhere in the undergrowth, thrown from a car window? Or, was the person who had taken Ellie keeping it? Did he switch it on from time to time? If it rang, did he switch it off quickly? Or did he listen to it ring? If he did, what would make him answer? Perhaps, if Dom left the right kind of message, whoever listened to it might call back. Her message box must either be full or nearly so. There wasn't much time left. There was a burst of incongruous laughter from the television show his parents were watching in the next room.

Dom took out his phone, put in Ellie's number and watched the call connect. Six rings, then the connection was broken. It didn't go to answer phone. It just stopped mid-tone. That meant that someone had pressed *end call*. Dom felt a lightness in his stomach. His palms began to sweat. Someone had waited, listening to the ring tone, had decided not to take the call. For some ridiculous reason, Dom felt a surge of new hope. There must be a way to make this person decide to answer, to accept his call. He just had to figure out how to make it happen.

It was difficult to resist the temptation to dial

again. But it was important to think. There may not be many more chances. It would be best to relax for a while, mull it over. So he got a beer from the fridge and went upstairs to his room. He clicked on the TV to watch 'The Hundred'. He and Ellie had watched the first few episodes together, sitting close on the sofa at her house. If he closed his eyes, he could still pick up the scent of her skin, her silky hair. He could sense the pressure of her hand, its fingers interlocked with his. And he made a promise to her and to himself. He would not give up. He would never lose hope. The thought of her house lying empty was unsettling. He had an urge to go over there. Her parents would probably want to talk, but he had already told them everything he knew, which wasn't much. The atmosphere would be loaded – it would do no one any favours.

He lit a cigarette. The police had other cases to work on. Everyday cases. Maybe they weren't as important, but they wouldn't stop just because a girl had gone missing in the town. Ellie's investigation would be filed before long, if nothing new turned up. Just another missing person. Dom had a sinking feeling that Alice Candy, despite her formidable record, already believed it was too late for Ellie.

Jaded. That's the word his dad had used about the inspector, when he'd seen her make her announcement on the news. Alice Candy had been in her job for too long, he'd said. She'd given up expecting the unusual, and convinced herself that there was an inevitable pattern to these things. That was what his dad had said. His dad watched too many police dramas on television. Dom wasn't sure he agreed with his assessment. In fact, if anyone looked jaded it was his father. Ellie's disappearance had hit him hard. No, Dom liked Alice Candy, with her defined facial features and no nonsense approach. She was not pretty, but certainly an attractive, strong woman. And there was something about her eyes. She was focused. She was intelligent. She would do her job well. But she was probably also a realist.

Dom sighed. He needed another beer. His parents were still in the lounge, but his mother would be fixing something to eat soon and he really didn't want to talk. He banged on the wall instead and called out, "Get me a beer, Ed?" There was the sound of a door opening followed by quick footsteps on the stairs. Moments later, Eddie popped his head around the door.

"I got you a cold one."

"Thanks, bro." Dom held out his hand and Eddie advanced tentatively. "You okay, Ed?"

The boy gave him an uncertain smile.

"It's going to work out. We'll find her."

The smile on Eddie's face grew a little larger, but lacked confidence.

"I promise...Now get out of here! Let me know when it's time to eat, okay?"

Eddie beamed and left the door open to run downstairs again. Dom heard him asking when dinner would be ready. The boy was hyperactive. In fact, the whole family was on tenterhooks, grabbing at any strand of normality. It was tough on all of them.

Getting up to close the door, Dom's thoughts returned to Ellie and he began to run through some of the outcomes there could be. One of them was that Ellie would be found alive and well as a result of the police investigation. Another was that she would escape. It was possible. She was a resourceful girl.

Still another was that he would find her, rescue her from her captor and hold her safe in his arms. This was the scenario he liked best.

Pulling his laptop from the table next to him he put in a search on *Google*. It brought up a list of text messages – the most irresistible cold call phrases, designed to incite action. Most of them were pathetic. He copied some he thought had potential into a word document: "You're a winner! Don't hang up." "We have important news for you, just call this number." Some of them were friendly, some professional, some pornographic. There were some that caught his interest more than others. If they caught *his* interest, then they might work on someone else. "What if this call were the only call you should have taken today?" or "I know you are there and I'm going to find you!" He particularly liked this last one. It reminded him of a film starring Liam Neeson. *I will find you, and I will kill you!* What if he used that one? Would it have an effect? After all, it was how he felt.

On the television, Jake Griffin was to be executed for letting everyone on the space station know that the food and air would soon run out unless half of the personnel volunteered to die. Jake Griffin thought this information should be shared. But his superiors thought it would cause panic and arrested him. His wife arrived too late to save him. Instead, she was forced to watch him being jettisoned into space. Nothing she could do to stop it happening. Nothing. If Ellie had been sitting next to Dom, she would have held his hand more tightly, and perhaps rested her head on his shoulder.

I'm going to find you, Ellie.

Dom closed his eyes and sent out the same thought, over and over again:

I'm going to find you.

Chapter Eight

Alice Candy was the last to leave, as usual. She took out her makeup bag and put on the lipstick she saved for the end of the day. Pale pink. It brought out the girl in her, someone had once said. He'd said she should grow her hair onto her shoulders and wear pretty, high-heeled shoes. There had been a few men like this one – none of them had worked out.

She eyed the closed file on her desk. She could probably recite most of it word for word. There would soon be pressure from above for Ellie Braintree's case to be moved to a lower level of priority, pending further information. If this happened, the likelihood of finding the girl would diminish. And, despite her best efforts, there didn't seem to be much more she could do. It was true that there was very little to go on, considering Ellie had been taken during the early afternoon and there must have been folk around. But people didn't notice what was going on under their noses, most of the time. Even worse, sometimes they invented detail and mis-remembered what their own eyes had seen.

That someone, somewhere had been nearby when Ellie had been taken - Alice Candy would bet her life on it. That the girl was being held close by was also likely. That she would be found was down to the efficiency of ongoing investigations, persistence, and luck.

Slipping on her jacket, the inspector left her office

and found Will, who was alone at his desk. She told him she was going to pay Mrs. Adams another visit.

"Shall I come with you, Boss?"

"No. No thank you, Will. You should finish up and go home."

"Nearly done," he replied.

He looked tired. His normally brilliant smile barely ignited. She laid a hand on his shoulder and left it there for a long moment, making sure and lucid eye contact, before walking away. Will could look after himself, she knew. Right now, she needed fresh air and time to think. This cliché ran back and forth inside her head and made her smile. Time to think. Fresh air. Were the two related?

Outside, the sun was still shining. The end of another pleasant summer's day. On just such a day, Ellie Braintree had visited the local shop and disappeared without a trace, as she made her way home. Someone must have seen something. Another cliché. This one brought to mind the witnesses who had come forward with earnest faces and careful, minute recollections that wandered around in circles and never hit the mark. Vagaries. Trivia. What was needed was just one watertight clue. That was all Alice Candy wanted. So far, the hours of reading and listening to statements, separating facts from blind, benevolent conjecture, had yielded precisely nothing.

There was a parking space right outside the shop. There were boxes ranged along the pavement with fresh produce sold at high prices. The door stood open invitingly. Inspector Candy looked up the road, picturing Ellie in the sunshine, moving away, preoccupied with her own thoughts. She caught the rhythm of her walk and the swinging of her carrier bag. Going home. Taking the short cut. There she went, past the pub on the left, the park on her right, turning now, onto the gravel path. And...gone.

Where did you go, Ellie?

There was still the faint odour of paint as she entered the shop, but no warning sign.

"Good evening, Mrs. Adams."

There were no other customers, but Mrs. Adams stood ready behind the counter, almost as though she had been expecting Alice Candy, or another customer to arrive at that precise moment. The two women exchanged a look.

"Good evening, Inspector. What can I do for you?"

Alice Candy glanced down. The confectionary tray was directly in front of her. "I'll take a *Crunchie* bar, please." *Old habits die hard*, she thought, remembering her own walk back from school past just such a corner shop when she'd been a child.

Mrs. Adams smiled pleasantly. She didn't ask about Ellie. That suited Alice Candy just fine. There wouldn't be anything new to say, anyway.

She paid for the chocolate. "Do you mind if I have another look around, Mrs. Adams?"

The shopkeeper met the inspector's gaze, hesitating for a moment, then nodded, regaining the pleasant tone she reserved for her customers. "Of course. Not in the slightest. Let me know if you need anything, won't you?"

The woman was curious, that was obvious, but she held herself in check, and Alice Candy respected her for it. Of course, there was something more. Something personal. The inspector knew what people like Rosemary Adams said about her. That she was psychic, a weirdo. That her husband had left her because of it. That she could track missing persons better than a sniffer dog. And there were stories. One above all: She had saved a boy's life by intervening in a domestic dispute. She had foreseen in a vision that the father would stab his son and had stepped in front of him at the precise moment before he had brought out the blade. It was rumoured that she had taken a deep wound to the stomach and still managed to arrest the man.

She thanked Mrs. Adams and turned to walk into the interior of the shop. It was relatively dark away from the counter despite the overhead strip lights. Up and down the aisles she wandered, making for the milk, then the bread. Ellie was there with her, as clear as could be, selecting a small cut loaf. In her other hand, a pint of skimmed milk. There was something else. What was it? Something that she had bought on a whim. *Are you thirsty, Ellie?* She thought.

Alice looked over to see Mrs. Adams pretending not to watch. She knew that, compared to Rosemary Adams, she looked stiff and formal. It was clear that the proprietor of the shop favoured a more casual appearance.

It came to her all of a sudden: Ellie had bought a can of drink. Alice Candy saw her put it on the counter. She needed no confirmation.

It was more from a sense of scientific interest that she sought to jog the shopkeeper's memory.

She approached the counter and said, "I'll take a can of lemonade, too."

The reply was automatic. No doubt repeated a hundred times a week. "I've got Sprite. Will that be all right?" And as she said it, it was evident that

Rosemary Adams remembered something.

"What is it, Mrs. Adams?" Alice Candy could recognise a moment of enlightenment as easily as the crash of a thunderbolt.

"Oh, it's probably not important. I just remembered that Ellie bought a can of Sprite on the day she..."

Even when unnecessary, confirmation was always gratifying. "I see. Thank you. It could be nothing, as you say, but I never take anything for granted in a case like this. The smallest clue could turn out to be of the utmost importance."

She observed Rosemary Adams bristle with awkward pride, as she took the inspector's money and wished her good evening.

Alice Candy turned to leave and had the strongest intuition yet that Ellie was alive and well. She couldn't suppress the wave of energy buzzing through her bones and so she followed it until it disappeared.

I'm coming for you, Ellie. Just hold on, girl.

Outside, the weather was perfect for sitting on the terrace of the King's Head and watching the world go by. If Ellie had come by a little later, there would have been people having a drink there.

As it was, she'd come out of the shop at around four-thirty – that was the time the magazine delivery had been made, and Mrs. Adams had remembered that Ellie had not minded waiting a moment while she completed the formalities with her supplier. Not all her customers would have been so understanding, she'd implied.

Four-thirty, or maybe a little later. There would have been no one at the pub. Inspector Candy pictured the empty tables, the sun higher in the sky. Light traffic. Before people came out of work.

There had been a few children at the recreation ground. Children playing after school. Their parents sitting chatting nearby. Those who had come forward hadn't seen anything out of the ordinary. One of the women thought she remembered a young girl passing by, but she couldn't say whether she had turned towards the allotments. She wouldn't have been able to see, from the park, anyway. Not from the benches. The turning was on the same side as the park, after a tall hedge that would have hidden Ellie's route from view.

Pausing for a moment, Alice Candy didn't have to close her eyes to picture the women laughing and gossiping with each other on the bench, or to hear the sounds of children squealing, riding the roundabout and laughing at the fun they were having.

Ellie's boyfriend had told the inspector that she invariably took the shortcut alongside the allotments. Invariably. It was a strange word, signifying imperfect knowledge. No better than guesswork. It was all there was to go on, and this kind of intimate knowledge was more reliable than most other conjecture. None of the owners had been on his or her allotment between four-thirty and five o'clock. This was very bad luck. Or very careful planning.

Alice Candy walked past the hedge and turned onto the path. It was a lovely place, with tall trees along one side: a single mature oak, and then birches, their top-most branches bending in the gentle breeze, their leaves flashing like fish under water. On the left, two men worked with their sleeves rolled up, one with a garden fork, the other amongst tomato plant canes.

The inspector sat on the concrete bench provided and opened her drink. The grass was cut short. Beneath her feet, it had been worn down to bare earth. A trail of ants was busy around one of the legs of the bench, disappearing and reappearing in endless scavenging activity. Very near to their nest, something caught Alice Candy's eye. It was a ring-pull from a drinks can, sticking half in and half out of the ground. The inspector was well aware that it was a long shot, but she took out a specimen bag anyway, collected the sliver of metal and sealed it inside, before slipping it into her pocket. Perhaps it had been missed, stuck under the bench like that. Just possible.

One of the men in his allotment saluted the tall, thin, elegant woman as she mulled over the facts of the case. She recognised him as one of several witnesses called in to give statements. Alice Candy raised a hand and smiled. It would be difficult for the owners of these pleasant gardens to feel quite the same about the place, now that a local girl had gone missing here. Unless this girl could be brought back alive and unharmed.

A sharp gust of wind shook the trees, making a sound like paper rustling, and beyond the allotments, the rose tinted sun sank lower over the gentle hills. It wouldn't be long before the shadows lengthened and the golden light that bathed the vegetable plots was extinguished. As colour drained from the world, intuition was strong in Alice Candy. This was where Ellie had sat, she was sure of it. What had happened to her next? It was tantalising to be so close to a new revelation, a deeper empathy. If only it would come. If it did not come now, it might well be lost for good. Losing an insight when it was so close could be disastrous.

In front and to her left was a pull-in for vehicles, presently unoccupied. There were tyre marks. Alice Candy concentrated. The image was unclear. A van of some kind. Bright. With lettering on the side. What did it say? She was almost there when, behind her, she heard the sound of a whisper. It came from far away but flowed slowly around her and into her head like insidious tentacles. *Hello Ellie*. And every hair on Alice Candy's body stood on end.

The moment passed quickly. She had not gleaned as much as she had hoped she would. What remained was the realisation that Ellie was in danger from someone who knew her name. That she had been taken by someone who knew her and meant her harm.

Walking back to her car, past the King's Head, the inspector was aware of a bus pulling up behind her. Turning, she saw two people get up from one of the pub's wooden picnic tables and heard the whoosh of doors opening. Alice Candy stopped abruptly, checked the time on her watch, then crossed the road to examine the bus timetable.

The number eight came along at half past the hour, every hour, every day except Sunday. The vehicle pulled away slowly and she watched as the passengers sitting on the driver's side looked out onto the allotments.

Chapter Nine

Ellie tried to use her time constructively. She'd deliberately held back from making rash moves. When the time was right, she would act. Staying positive was essential. But sometimes her thoughts were darker. She must not give in to them.

After a session of vigorous exercise, she washed her face in the sink and wished she had a mirror. The smallest of luxuries – being able to straighten her hair, or check her face, were denied to her. Then, she was drawn away from practicalities into the far more dangerous world of 'what ifs'. What if this were to be her life from now on? The answer shot back at her: *At least she would be alive.* Then another thought struck Ellie. *What if something happened to the man who brought her tray? And what if he were the only person in the world who knew she was locked away in this cellar?* This was a line of questioning she had no desire to follow.

Ever the optimist, Ellie preferred to look on the bright side. Even in her present predicament there were things to be grateful for. She had a lamp now. She had magazines, plenty of writing and drawing paper. She had two dressing gowns, the clothes she had been wearing, washed and ironed, and two blankets. Today, the fifth day, there'd been an MP3 player with headphones on the tray, and she'd been surprised to find most of her favourite songs on it, until she realised that they must have been copied from her phone. That meant they'd got past the password. She should have made a stronger one.

The man had coughed again today. This time, as though he were not well. And, racked with half imagined, half plausible catastrophes, Ellie had come to a decision: she would try again to get out, the next time he came. Rushing him had been no good, she'd only tried it once, but had not been quick enough. She had bided her time, but eventually had acted on impulse, leaping up and making a grab for the door. Now he would be on his guard.

No, next time she had to be more cunning. After a great deal of deliberation, Ellie had come up with an alternative plan. It might work, it might not. The only way she would find out would be to give it a go. So, she dragged her bed to the other side of the room, where it could not be seen from the door. Now it was a question of waiting. There was a chance that, if she kept very quiet, he would worry that something was wrong. If he could not see her, he might be curious. And she would be near enough to get to the door before he closed it. It would give her a chance to get past him. Just a chance.

Sitting on the re-positioned bed, trying to contain her trepidation, she read for a while, until she estimated it might be time for a visit, then she moved to one end of the bed, close to the door, and waited in silence. Soon enough, she heard a faint click at the other end of the passageway and sensed rather than heard him approaching. Sometimes, something on the tray rattled. She'd once thought she'd heard his footsteps but finally believed she had mistaken them for the beating of her heart. Ellie had concluded that the man had to be wearing soft shoes, walking on

51

carpet or more likely bare earth. Today, she heard nothing, until he reached the door. He had never opened the sliding door behind the window, preferring, she presumed, to search her out through the hole, three quarters of the way up. Before the arrival of the lamp, he would have needed good vision to see her clearly. Ellie cursed herself for not having tried this trick earlier, and she cursed herself even more now for having left the lamp on. Too late to switch if off. Damn!

He must be looking. She held her breath. Then she heard something. It wasn't much. Just the lightest of touches, and she knew instantly that the door would not open. Normally, there would be the sound of the key slipping into the lock, a pause to double check that she was still on the bed, the key turning, the latch lifting, and then the quick slide of the tray, before the door clanked shut again. If there was anything to collect, it would be done in the middle of the night. She put washing inside a black plastic bag and positioned it to the side of the door. If it were not close enough, he didn't take it. The same with the bucket.

The silence now was ambiguous. It was impossible to know whether he was still outside. Ellie held her breath, but there was no clue until she heard a cough in the distance. He had not opened up. He had not left the tray. Very well, she would wait. She had water and a stock of food. She would not be the first to give in.

Chapter Ten

Dom activated the new phone and dialled Lou's number. He should start with the least susceptible of his friends. Lou would never answer her phone if it were not someone she knew. She wouldn't recognise the number. She would not answer. Sure enough, he heard it cut off and go to answer phone. "Leave a message if I know you. If I don't, please don't bother me again."

Here goes, thought Dom. "This might be a call you really ought to take." Did his voice sound different enough?

Lou didn't take the bait. She didn't pick up. She didn't call back.

Next, he plugged in Paul's number. From one extreme to the other.

"Hey!"

"What if I told you I know where you are?"

"Eh? Who is this?" Paul was already expecting a prank.

Dom didn't speak, stifling a laugh.

"Quit it! I know it's you, Junker! You are *such* a moron!" He laughed a hoot of a laugh.

Dom bit his lip.

"Who are you talking to, Pauly? Get back over here!" said Jen in the background.

He came clean. "It's not Junker, it's Dom. Can I come over?"

"Er..."

"...Not right now, obviously. But it's about Ellie. I want to try something, and I want your help."

"What about Ellie? Is there some news?" Paul suddenly sounded more alert.

Jen grabbed the phone then, and they both insisted that he come over immediately.

"Bring wine. Oh, and chocolate," said Jen.

It was late, but Dom was so full of the thought of actually doing something that he drove straight over, calling in at the late-night supermarket on the way. Jen and Paul were waiting outside.

"Brrr! Come inside, it's cold." They were still wearing shorts and tee shirts.

"What are you waiting outside for? And what's with the floral shorts?"

"Just get in and tell us what's going on."

They worked for the next couple of hours, thinking up what to say, calling up friends, testing out their best lines. In the end they settled on three that seemed to work best and decided to try one of them out the next day.

"It's late, we're tired. We might not be so convincing if we do it now," said Paul.

Dom still held on to his phone.

"Come on, Pauly. Why don't we try it?" said Jen. "We might be better while the idea is fresh. While we're slick, you know?"

"Really?" Paul wasn't convinced.

"Maybe Jen's right," said Dom. "Tomorrow it might seem like a stupid idea." In fact, he didn't like to think of Ellie having to wait a minute longer than she had to.

"You said it!" replied Paul.

Jen gave Paul a look. She held her hand out for Dom's phone. "Are *you* going to do it? Or d'you want *me* to?"

"Maybe *I* should do it," replied Dom.

"D'you think he's more likely to pick up for Jen or for you?" Paul looked from one to the other.

"It'll probably be switched off, anyway," said Dom.

"Maybe we *should* wait," said Jen.

"No. I'm going to try." Dom selected 'record conversation', put in Ellie's number and listened. After the fifth ring tone it connected. There was no answer phone message. That was strange. He listened, hardly daring to breathe, then spoke. "I know who you are and I know how to find you."

Silence.

Paul and Jen stared.

"You have twenty-four hours to return my call."

Then, someone spoke, but Dom couldn't make out the words. There was something, but it was muffled, then there was a cough, followed by another, then nothing. It was Dom who pressed 'end call'. His hands were shaking.

"He answered?" Jen was still staring.

"Yes."

"What did he say?"

"It was really unclear. I couldn't catch it."

"Bloody hell, Dom."

"He coughed, twice."

The three of them listened to the call over and over again. In the background, there was the sound of traffic. Was there a voice? In the end Paul decided there was, from the rhythm, if nothing else.

"We should take it to the police," said Jen. They

have special equipment for picking up sound and amplifying it. There might be other things they can pick out that we can't hear, too."

"If we go to the police, they'll take over," said Dom. "I think we should wait and see whether he calls back. I said twenty-four hours. Let's see what he does."

"I don't know, Dom. Maybe it's risky to wait. Who knows what he might do. He might panic and..."

"Isn't there anyone you could trust to help us?" asked Paul.

Dom thought of Alice Candy. "There might be one person."

Chapter Eleven

Ellie was in a deep sleep, dreaming about the night she had met Dom. He'd been sitting on his own in the corner of a nightclub, while the music blared out and people danced. Every now and then the lights from the DJ's deck would slide over his face. His eyes were cast down, his elbows on his knees, head in his hands. Ellie couldn't work out whether he was drunk, tired or just down.

Here came the light, illuminating his jaw, his cheekbones, his high forehead. Then, he looked at her. Full on, with those huge, sexy eyes.

Ellie woke with a start. It took her a moment to realise where she was. Then, she knew that, in the darkness, something had changed. She sat up in bed, breathing heavily, fumbling for her lamp.

"Who…who's there?" Her voice was choked and her body trembled violently. She grabbed her pillow and held it in front of her, at the same time, locating the lamp and switching it on. Her pulse was racing. *This is it*! she thought. *He's in the room. This is it!*

Then, she heard a noise, a pitiful, quiet sobbing, coming from the other side of the room. She stood up and moved forward with the pool of light from the lamp before her, illuminating her bare feet. The carpet ended. She wanted her slippers but couldn't go back. The dirt was gritty and raw. Ellie shivered. Then, she saw her – sitting on the dank earth, squeezed into the corner next to the washbasin. A girl.

All Ellie could see at first was the circle of golden shine from the blond hair on top of her head, and the shocking whiteness of her bare legs.

"Don't hurt me, please," whimpered the girl. "Don't hurt me."

The lamplight was harsh. White, not yellow, so that the girl's flesh was tinged with a cold blue aura. The round of her face, now she looked up, framed so perfectly by her neat hair, which Ellie saw was cut into a bob, shone out like a frozen planet against the night sky. Makeup had left a black trail beneath each eye and there was snot running from her nose, saliva from her mouth. Still she trembled, pushing herself further into the corner, curling up into a ball.

Ellie set the lamp down and held out a hand. The girl looked from her face to the proffered hand and back again, finally reaching out to take it.

"My name's Ellie."

"What... what is this place?" The girl could barely speak.

Ellie remembered how disoriented she'd felt when she'd awoken, alone and terrified of the earth beneath her body and the darkness all around.

"Don't worry. I'll help you. Let me get a cloth for your face."

The girl wiped away the stains and sighed long and deep. Her sobbing abated a little, but her eyes were full of terror, still.

"Did you see who took you?" asked Ellie, gently.

"Did he take you, too?"

"Yes. But I didn't see his face."

The girl shook her head and seemed to be disgusted as she described her attacker. "He was old. Over fifty, I'd say. Ugly. He had no hair and a big nose, long like a fox." She let out a strangled sob before continuing. "He seemed ordinary. Nice. He asked me for directions." She laughed a little. But it was laden with derision. "The oldest trick in the book, eh?"

Ellie took her hand again. The girl must still be in shock.

"Can you stand up? There's a bed over here.

"Do you sleep here?"

"Yes."

"Why?"

"The door is locked."

The girl took this simple fact in, her eyes wide.

"Ellie?"

"Yes."

"How long have you been here?"

"I think I've been here seven days. There's a very narrow gap at the top of the wall, so I know when it's daytime, but I don't know what time it is."

The girl sat on the bed and Ellie realised that her wrists had not been bound, neither had her shoes been taken. She was wearing a long sleeved pullover that was too big for her, some cut-off jeans and what looked like expensive cross-trainers.

"Are you cold?"

"No. I'm all right." The girl gave Ellie a half smile.

"Here, drink this."

She drank some of the water Ellie handed her. Then she smiled more broadly. "I'm Donna. Thanks."

"Don't worry, Donna. We'll get out of here. I'm sure of it." Ellie only half believed what she was saying. She hoped that Donna would at least have *some* confidence in her promise.

There had been no food delivered for some time, and Ellie had survived on biscuits and fruit. The little that remained, she offered to Donna.

It was a profound comfort to have the company of another person. Ellie couldn't help feeling a new glow of optimism, but, at the same time, she wondered what this new arrival meant. Was he collecting girls? Would he deliver more food? Should she move her bed back, so that he would return with the trays?

She'd heard about 'snuff' movies and how people were captured, put in extreme situations and filmed for the entertainment of a remote audience desperate for sadistic satisfaction. Sick people. Would she and Donna be left to slowly starve? Would people watch them die, mewling like children in the dark? The thought was infinitely terrifying and infinitely sad. Her family would probably never find her. Her body would rot. Her bones would remain as a testament to her suffering, to be discovered in years to come. And now, there was Donna, too. It could not happen! Not like this!

Together, they moved the bed back so that it could be seen from the door. So that he could know where they were and bring them food. Donna didn't ask why they were moving the bed, she just followed Ellie's lead. The poor girl would need to rest, after her ordeal. They would talk later.

As soon as the bed had been replaced, food came again. No second bed arrived and so the girls slept head to toe at first, but soon, Donna crawled in next to Ellie, and they slept in each other's arms.

When the next tray had arrived, there was fresh fruit, yoghurt, two burgers and two cans of coke.

"Mmm. I'm hungry!" said Donna. "Let's eat."

She didn't hesitate for a second. Only when she saw Ellie looking at her, did she stop chewing.

"Oh, do you think it's all right to eat?"

Ellie's frown vanished. "What choice do we have? It hasn't killed me yet." All the same, it was a little surprising that Donna hadn't even thought about the possibility of the food being unsafe. Ellie didn't tell her that she suspected the food was drugged sometimes.

"Here," said Donna, passing Ellie one of the burgers, "it's a McDonalds."

Ellie bit into it. It was delicious. And still quite hot. That must mean they were near a town. A town with a McDonalds in it.

"Want a napkin?" asked Donna.

Ellie took the one she offered. Would there be an address, a clue of some kind? She put down her burger.

"What are you doing?"

"Checking - there might be a clue, you know, as to where we are." Then she saw it. Stuck to the bottom of Donna's burger. A slip of paper. "Wait! Give me your burger."

Donna stared. "What is it?"

Ellie carefully peeled away the piece of paper, damp from its contact with the warm bun.

"A receipt."

With the lamp held close, they could make out a time, a date and an amount. And there, at the top, where the paper was torn, part of an address.

"Let me see." Donna took the piece of paper, carefully. "Where are we looking?"

"At the... Donna! No! Now you've got ketchup on it!"

Donna was quiet after they'd eaten. She didn't want to talk. She'd said she was sorry and then complained that she was very tired.

Ellie was sorry she had snapped at her over the ruined receipt. She lay down and closed her eyes, listening to Donna's quiet breathing. Later, when Ellie pushed back the blanket and sat up, Donna awoke and asked what she was doing.

"I want to send him a message."

She sat up. "What are you going to say?"

"That he should talk to us. Tell us why we are here."

"He won't do that." Donna's laugh was derisory.

Ellie put down her pen and looked at her. "He might. After all, he hasn't harmed us. I think he's a timid person. I think he's confused and maybe even frightened."

"How can you know all this? You might make him angry."

"I don't think so. He's always given me what I've asked for. I think he's a kind person."

"Not everything. He hasn't given you everything you've asked for."

Ellie looked at Donna and waited for an explanation.

"I mean, he hasn't let you go, has he?"

Ellie remembered asking for real light. Daylight. She hadn't actually asked him to let her go. Or had she?

"I mean, he must know that you don't want to stay locked up. It stands to reason."

It seemed to Ellie that Donna was being unnecessarily obstructive. She was still scared. It had taken Ellie quite a while to think rationally.

"Listen, Donna. I've been here a long time. Long

enough to learn stuff about him, even though he doesn't speak or show his face."

"What stuff?"

"Well, I've seen how he pushes in the tray. Even though I must stay on my bed. It's not done in an aggressive way. His hand is small, and his arm is almost parallel to the ground, which means he crouches down. Down low."

"So?"

"So he seems wary, not uncaring. And I think he must be young - or at least not old. Otherwise he would be more confident, more decisive. He might use his foot, so as not to have to get down low. Just shove the tray inside. Give it a kick. Don't you think?"

"No. *I'd* use my foot, if it was *me*. And *I'm* young."

"He holds on to the door with one hand, I've seen his fingers, and pushes the tray in with the other."

"How can you see all this in the dark?"

"I put the lamp behind the door, on a low setting. I don't think he knows. His eyes aren't as used to the dark as mine are."

Donna stared, her eyes wide. "Wow! You've really done your homework, haven't you, Ellie?"

"I just think…"

"So he's shy. So, how does that help us?"

"Well, that's not all. He cares that we are comfortable."

"He left you without food when you moved the bed! How is that caring?"

Ellie hesitated. Then she took a different tack. "He makes mistakes, Donna. The receipt, for example."

"I still don't see how..."

63

"We can use it. Don't you see? To undermine his confidence. You know, tell him we know things. Worry him. But first, I want to try a more direct approach."

Ellie wrote the note and pushed it under one of the paper plates.

"And that's another thing. Why does he give us plates and napkins? You know, it seems to me sometimes that he's trying too hard. Like a child, or someone who doesn't quite know what to do."

"You sound like a psychologist, or something." Donna drew her legs up and rested her chin on her knees. She reached out and pushed a stray strand of hair away from Ellie's eyes. "Anyway, aren't you forgetting that I told you - I *saw* him. He didn't seem shy to me. He seemed scary. He made me do as he said, and locked me in the back of his van. He was big. And rough. He wasn't young and stupid."

Ellie hesitated once more. "I never said he was stupid, Donna."

The girls didn't speak for a moment. Then Ellie had a thought. "How did he get you into the van?"

"What?"

"I mean, when he asked you for directions?"

"He...he twisted my arm behind my back and said he'd hurt me if I didn't do as I was told. It was all so quick. I was so scared, Ellie." Donna put her head down. Her shoulders began to shake.

"Where did he stop you? And where did he ask directions to?" Ellie wanted answers.

Just then, the door opened and the old tray slid out. For a moment, the door remained ajar, but by the time Ellie had jumped up, it had closed again.

Ellie listened, then whispered, "I didn't hear a key,

did you?"

"What?"

"Usually, he puts a key in the lock and turns it, twice. He didn't this time."

Ellie tried the door. It was firm. But it would be, if the latch were down.

"I wonder..." said Ellie, crouching down and looking through the keyhole.

For some reason, she kept her next thoughts to herself. Perhaps Donna wasn't ready to make a move. Perhaps she was still nervous, afraid of what might happen if they tried to escape. Staring out at the darkness on the other side of the door, Ellie began to form a plan. *Maybe he forgot to lock it. Maybe he panicked and didn't use the key. Maybe, just maybe, she would be able to push up the latch on the other side and open the door.*

Chapter Twelve

Alice Candy was sitting opposite a corpulent, well dressed woman wearing a worried expression, and clutching the hand of the boy who sat next to her.

Their initial statement had not revealed much, but in the last few minutes, the boy had been most helpful. He hadn't spoken freely for the constable who had taken the original statement, his mother told Inspector Candy, because he had been scared. Inspector Candy had explained the situation much better, she said, so that Cedric could understand how important it would be to tell the police exactly what he saw.

The phone lit up as Mrs. Werrel was summing up, for the third time, what a useful experience this had been for Cedric and, as there was little more in the way of usable content to note down, Alice Candy excused herself with a nod and a half smile, and picked up the call.

"Sorry to interrupt, Inspector. There's a gentlemen in reception who says he has information on the Ellie Braintree case. He says it's urgent."

Dom was escorted upstairs and left outside the inspector's office. He knocked on the half glazed door and went in to find Alice Candy sitting behind her desk with the lights out. Her eyes were closed but she was not asleep. A strange odour of paper and dust hung about the place.

"I don't like the cleaners to come in," she said, her eyes opening slightly. "They always move things around. Take a seat Mr. Bryant."

Dom experienced a sinking feeling and wished he hadn't come. The whole place exuded an air of stagnation.

"I hear you have something to tell me?"

He was a little surprised by the directness of the inspector's question. He hadn't yet made up his mind how much to tell her. "I... I don't know whether it's anything, really. I ..."

Alice Candy seemed to sense his reticence and, holding his gaze, gave him the distinct impression that she would extract the information he had brought with him whether he liked it or not.

It was clear from her words that she was willing to trade. "I want you to know, Mr. Bryant, that the investigation is ongoing. I am in the process of following up fresh leads on Ellie's case. We have a new witness."

He waited for Alice Candy to go on, but she didn't.

"What is it you have for me?" she repeated.

Dom took out his phone and handed it to the inspector.

"Listen to the last call I made. I recorded it."

Alice Candy remained composed, as they listened to his dramatic introduction followed by his theatrical threat. In between, there was definitely something. The quality was not great, though, and in the office, it seemed as though there was nothing much to hear at all.

"Can you... Have you got equipment to enhance ..."

"When did you make this call, Mr. Bryant?"

"Last night. At about eleven-fifteen."

"May I keep your phone for the time being?"

"Yes. For how long, though?""

"Is this your personal phone? I mean is this your regular phone? Or did you purchase it specifically?"

It was oddly impressive that this woman knew the exact question to ask.

It's new. I thought he wouldn't pick up if he knew it was me...if Ellie had told him who I was."

Alice Candy nodded and, if he wasn't mistaken, smiled.

"I'll get it back to you soon and we can discuss what to do from there."

"Do you think you can trace Ellie's phone's location?"

"Let me see what we can get from the recording, first. Thank you for bringing this to me, Mr. Bryant. If there's nothing more…"

He was being dismissed. Dom got up to leave.

"You'll be contacted when we've analysed the recording. And, Mr. Bryant, it might be prudent not to try to contact Ellie, or whoever might have her phone, again until we learn more."

Alice Candy watched the young man walk away from her office, his shoulders rounded, his head down. The move had been a rash one, and he knew it. It was impossible to know whom they were dealing with yet. At the same time, the inspector understood completely. Dominic Bryant was desperate. He and his friends had come up with an idea and had gone ahead without thinking.

The phone was in the hands of someone who was not Ellie. For days the special unit team had tried to trace it, but the phone had been switched off. Why then, at eleven-fifteen the previous night had it been switched on? It was probable that the kidnapper had disposed of it. It was probable that someone else had discovered it in a litterbin, or thrown away on the side of the road. It was probable that this person would change the SIM card and keep the phone. Finders keepers. There was a small chance that the phone would be handed in, especially if the person who'd found it realised who it belonged to. There was an even smaller chance that the person who'd answered the call last night was Ellie's kidnapper. And if it was, why had he picked up? If Alice Candy could hear his voice, listen to him, perhaps she might understand more. Perhaps.

The phone was taken down to Jerome Blaize for analysis. If there were anything on it, Jerome would find it. The inspector doubted whether there would be anything useful, though. Probably just the sound of someone breathing or grunting. After all, this was not like in the movies, where background noise could reveal the exact location of the victim. Where a train announcement had been picked up, or the idiosyncratic striking of a clock. No, this was real life. And in real life, there was not always a happy ending. The police sometimes got there too late, in real life. In real life, the police didn't manage to get there at all some of the time.

Right now, there was a new lead to follow up: Cedric Werrel, when his mother had given him a chance to speak, had described a yellow van with a blue stripe down its side and a telephone number ending in three-three-two. There had been something written above the number, but it had been obscured by bushes. Cedric thought one of the letters was an 's' and that the word had ended with a 't'. The van had been parked at the entrance to the allotments, perpendicular to the path that Ellie would have taken on her way home. No one else had seen the van, but Cedric had seemed like a reliable witness. Children were often more observant than adults, after all. The main thing was that it was something concrete to go on. Alice Candy remembered the tyre tracks she had seen when she had discovered the ring-pull and heard someone speak Ellie's name. This could be the breakthrough she'd been waiting for. And how many yellow vans could there be in the area, with a telephone number ending in three-three-two?

The inspector closed her eyes and took herself back to the bench once more. To the place where Ellie had sat drinking her can of Sprite. She saw the van amongst the trees, just visible from the road. What business did it have being there? How long had it stayed? It had still been light, the kidnapper had been careless – he must have known someone might notice a brightly coloured vehicle, even if it were mostly hidden from the road and parked next to empty allotments. If he had been careless once, he might have made other mistakes too. If he had, Alice Candy was going to uncover them. Let there be no doubt about that.

During the next few hours, while forensics re-examined what remained of the tyre tracks, thoughts went round in Alice Candy's head. The road was not a busy one, neither was it deserted. Why had the kidnapper not chosen a different spot? Why had he taken Ellie in daylight hours? It was true that no one was working on the allotments at the time. Had he known this? How could he know this? Was it luck, or good planning? Had he known that Ellie would come by? Or had he watched her house and driven ahead when she came out, following her to the shop and then lying in wait? Or had Ellie been a random victim? In the wrong place at the wrong time? *Hello Ellie. Hello Ellie.* The inspector knew that her intuition was not always reliable, but something told her that this time she was not mistaken. The kidnapper knew Ellie Braintree. Knew her with an intimate knowledge. This had been a planned attack.

A call had been put out to local patrols to look out for any vehicle resembling Cedric Werrel's description. No public announcement would be made yet. If the kidnapper had used his own vehicle, it would be hidden somewhere or would more likely have been disguised in some way. Perhaps with a change of plates, or even a re-spray. Actions that could be traced, with time and enough manpower.

There were good people doing a search of telephone numbers ending with three-three-two and running programmes with words that had an 's' in the middle and a 't' at the end. The phrase 'long shot' came to Alice Candy. But she knew that a long shot was better than no shot at all.

If she were alive, Ellie would be counting on someone getting her out of the situation she was in. By all accounts, she was a strong, independent type. She would need to be. Statistically, murders happened within the first twenty-four hours, after that, you knew you were dealing with an unbalanced mind. People who wanted to keep their victims alive for their own twisted purposes. These cases were rare. Alice Candy had only been involved in one other similar kidnapping. A young boy, one of three, had been on his way home from school. When he didn't arrive home, his mother had reported him missing. The team had been close, but not close enough to solving the case. It had been a terrible ordeal for everyone. The difference was that she had known from the start that the boy was dead. That all three had not survived longer than a few hours in the company of their abductor.

This time, it was not the same. Not the same at all. Alice Candy pictured Ellie alone, taking one moment at a time, trying to keep calm and hoping for the best. Ellie, in darkness. Darkness could mean that it was already too late. But there was a strong sense of energy, too. Ellie was alive. And, after so many days, intervention was her best hope. She should not try to escape. Not unless she could do it on the first attempt. Escape was only an option at the beginning, when the kidnapper wanted to prolong his pleasure. With the passing of time would come more complex feelings. Ellie would become a problem. A problem that was difficult to solve. It would become necessary to get rid of her. "Be careful, Ellie," the inspector murmured. "Don't try anything risky. Not now."

When the telephone rang, Alice Candy said she would come right away. Jerome had got something. A man's voice, and a name. Game on!

Chapter Thirteen

"Does Jessie want some chicken?"

In the warm kitchen, a Norfolk terrier cocked its head to one side. It had a pink ribbon tied inexpertly to a tuft of hair between its ears, and a red felt coat around its middle.

"Nice chicken, Jess. Look. The best bits. Shh! Don't tell." The young man put a hand over his mouth to suppress a giggle. There was a film of sweat on his upper lip, which he wiped away with a handkerchief pulled from a pocket. He wore jeans that were rather big for him, pulled up too high, and a checked shirt with the first button open. He moved awkwardly, with excessive care. His hair was dark, cut short and parted in the middle so that he resembled an office clerk in a Victorian novel. Heavily built and on the short side, he was not an attractive figure, but his face was kind and his tone of voice gentle.

The room was too warm. The stove was a wood burner and it was sending out copious amounts of heat. Too much for a late August afternoon. On the large farmhouse table there was a breadboard, half a loaf, a bread knife, some butter and a jar of honey. The young man opened the fridge again and, screwing up his face, peered inside.

"Oh dear, Jess."

The little dog came to his side, seeming to scan the contents of the fridge with his master. There was half a pint of milk, a bowl of eggs, two pots of yoghurt and a second unopened block of butter.

The young man went into the hall and came back wearing a jacket, even though his forehead too was now shining with perspiration. He took a bunch of keys from the sideboard and he glanced at the expensive-looking phone that lay on top of a bicycle repair book for beginners. He licked his lips. Not because he found the idea of the phone delicious, but because he was desperate not to make a bad decision. It would be safer to take it with him. No, no. It would be safer to leave it where it was. As long as it was turned off.

Make sure it's turned off, Joe. Understand? The police can't trace it if it's turned off.

It was red. Smooth and red. Cherry red. A thing of beauty, especially when it lit up. That happened when someone called. But only when it was switched on.

Make sure it's turned off, Joe. Understand?

It was turned off. If he pushed the button on the side, it played a tune and some words came up on the screen. To be sure it was off, he turned it on. Yes. Look. That was on. He held the phone, watching it come to life, feeling its cool sleekness in his palm. Clever. Like a miracle. No wires, no cables. Magic.

Don't do anything stupid, will you, Joe?

Joe didn't like that word. *Stupid!* He didn't like the sound it made, or the way people looked when they said it. Hurriedly, he pushed the button again and the phone lay dark and still in his hand. He knew the password. He'd overheard it. It was dangerous knowledge and he wished he could forget it. But he wouldn't use it. No, of course he wouldn't.

Opening the door, he turned and smiled. "See you soon, Jessie. Be good."

When Joe returned, he put the new supplies on the table and hurriedly inserted yet more wood into the stove (*keep the fire ticking over, Joe*) and set about putting away the shopping. *Ticking over*. The kitchen clock said it was almost dinnertime. *Ticking over*. So he got out the tray, wiped it down, even though it was already clean, and put two napkins at one side, folded neatly. He laid out strips of chicken from the new pack he'd opened and Jess fixed him with her doggy stare.

"No, Jess. No more for you tonight. Uh, uh. Greedy Jess!" He laughed.

Three strips each, with one left over. After a moment's hesitation, he cut the last strip in two as exactly as he could, popping one half into his mouth and tossing the other one to Jess.

"Sh! Don't tell, Jess."

On each plate, he arranged three cherry tomatoes, three slices of cucumber, a piece of buttered Hovis and a dollop of ketchup. The ketchup he looked at for some time, frowning, eventually trying to scoop it up and finally pulling out two new plates and starting from scratch, this time finishing off with a squirt of low fat mayonnaise and some lettuce leaves. Better. To the tray he added two fat-free strawberry yoghurts and two cans of sugar-free lemon Fanta. Ready. He balanced the tray and opened a door leading out of the kitchen, but not into the yard, nor into the interior of the house.

"Stay there, Jess. Stay! Good girl," he whispered.

The cooler air was refreshing. The smell of earth, pleasant. Joe took note of the steps down to the cellar. They were worn away in the middle, which made the descent a little precarious in the relative darkness. The light switch was on the wall just to the left, but Joe didn't use it (*keep the lights out, Joe*). He had, however, left the light in the kitchen on and the door open. When Joe looked back, he saw Jess sitting at the top of the steps.

"Shh! Quiet, Jessie," he whispered, grinning nervously.

The passageway was clear. Joe had removed all the junk. Mostly old furniture and broken bicycles. The furniture, he had burned in the yard, and the bicycles, he'd put to one side in the barn. When he had time he liked to clean them up and rebuild them. He took his book with him, but really didn't need it any more. And he didn't like to turn the pages when his hands were dirty. When he had delivered the tray perhaps he would sit in the kitchen and look at the wonderful pictures and read the clear instructions.

As he approached the cellar, goosebumps rose on his arms. It was different now that there were two guests in the cellar room. Joe felt less in control. Less confident. But he hoped that Ellie would feel more at home now that Donna was there to keep her company.

At the door, he set down the tray and stooped to look through the peephole. Ellie's bed was back where it should be and, now there was a lamp, it was much easier to see that she was sitting on one end, with Donna lying on her front behind her. They were talking. Joe watched them as he listened.

"We've been together for almost a year," said Ellie.

Donna rolled over onto her back and put her hands behind her head.

"What's he like?"

"Oh, I think he's just about perfect."

"Really? That sounds deadly!"

The girls laughed.

"Anyway, if he's so wonderful, he must look pretty bad." Donna was staring at Ellie.

Joe stared too.

Ellie grinned. She looked very pretty.

Donna rolled her eyes, then laughed again. "Come on! There must be something you don't like about him!"

Ellie didn't say anything. She looked as though she were thinking about something. Something outside the cellar room.

Joe licked his lips. He should open the door and push in the tray. It wasn't polite to listen to other people's private conversations. But he wanted to know about Dom – this person who was so wonderful. This person who loved Ellie. He licked his lips again, and saw that Donna was going to say something more.

"Tell me what's so special about him!"

Joe swallowed hard.

"I don't know. It's difficult to say what someone's like, isn't it?"

"Try."

"Okay. So, he's kind. He's gentle. He's clever."

"Boring!"

Joe frowned. Why was being kind, gentle and clever boring? And why were Donna and Ellie laughing again?

Ellie sighed. "Okay. He's tall with shoulder-length surfer-blond hair and amazing eyes. People say he looks like Heath Ledger."

"Oh, yeah. 'A Knight's Tale'. Better. And what does Prince Charming do all day?"

Ellie looked down at her hands. "He works. He's a teacher. Doing his probationary year."

"Oh, my God! Dull!"

"But in his free time, he swims."

"Yeah?"

"Yes. For the county. He's top of his class in butterfly."

"Impressive!"

Ellie put her head down.

Donna reached up and put a hand in the middle of Ellie's back. "Don't let this place get to you, Ellie. You'll see him again soon."

"How? How are we going to get out of here?"

Joe clasped the key and turned it in the lock the way he always did, but this time it met no resistance. Hesitating for a moment and checking the peephole – the girls didn't seem to know he was there – he lifted the latch and pushed the door open. The girls stopped speaking abruptly, and he quickly slid the tray into the room. Confused and a little shaken to have been party to their conversation, Joe wanted nothing more than to enter the room and show himself. He may not be handsome, he may not be clever, but he believed he was kind and gentle. Perhaps he should just walk in and introduce himself… But that would be stupid.

Don't do anything stupid, will you Joe?

He jerked the door closed, pushed down the heavy latch, put the key in the lock and turned it the wrong way. It didn't feel right, but he could not stay. Withdrawing the key, he pushed on the door – it felt firm. Almost breaking into a run, Joe made his way back to the kitchen, where Jess was waiting for him. He stooped to pick up the small dog and stood for a long moment gazing back along the long dark corridor that led to the cellar, stroking Jess and murmuring softly.

Chapter Fourteen

The yellow van with the blue stripe down the side and the telephone number ending in three-three-two was owned by Martin Eade, and mainly driven by his wife. They ran a market garden business, with their son, Andrew. 'Fast and Efficient'. There were the 's' and the 't'. On the line below: 'Service'. Well done, Cedric.

Alice Candy got out of the car and didn't wait for Will, who was tying a shoelace. The drive was muddy, with puddles that looked as though they rarely dried out. The house itself stood to one side with its front door wide open. There was no front garden, although a selection of pots containing more or less drowned plants, gave an impression that, at some point in time, someone had at least made an effort to create some kind of kerb appeal. To the other side of the driveway, was a covered yard, sheltering several enormous stacks of wooden pallets, a medium sized lorry and a yellow van.

Alice looked around for someone to speak to. From the back of the house, a Collie dog came forward, nose down, shoulders hunched, and behind it, a young man of around twenty-five, wearing a ripped tee shirt in need of laundering, and a pair of what may have been designer Levis. He wiped his hands on a towel, which was tucked into his belt, as he approached.

"Good morning," he said, holding out a still dirty

hand for Alice Candy to shake. "You can park on the hard standing, if you like." He indicated a large area of concrete, partially occupied by a Mercedes sports car. The amusement in his voice was not meant to offend.

Alice smiled at the affable young man. "Good morning. Inspector Alice Candy. I assume you are Andrew Eade."

"That's me."

Will Brady came forward and repeated the formalities. The inspector looked back at the car they had arrived in and wondered whether there was any point in moving it.

"I'll do it," said Will, looking down at his very muddy shoes and grinning.

Alice Candy gave him the keys.

"Dad's inside, if you'd like to talk to him." Andrew stood to the side, putting out an arm.

"Right," Alice Candy replied, stepping gingerly and wincing at the way DC Brady was crunching gears.

Inside, there was a large hall, with an adjoining utility room. There were neat rows of Wellington boots, pegs hung with coats and jackets for every season, and two dog's bowls, one empty and one with water in it. Two noisy, industrial-sized washing machines were making it difficult to hold a conversation.

"Sorry," said Andrew.

"Must be dirty work?" shouted Will Brady, who had just come in and handed Alice her keys.

"What? Oh, that's just my mum. She likes to keep things separate. House and farm, you know?"

Will nodded.

"Come through to the kitchen. Dad's probably got the kettle on."

"And Mrs. Eade?"

"Mum's doing deliveries until twelve."

"Deliveries?" asked Will.

Alice Candy looked the other way, towards the interior of the house.

"Veggie boxes. Big business."

Inside the large kitchen, a clock chimed half past eleven, and steam rose from a large old-fashioned kettle. Mr. Eade, a surprisingly slight man, with prominent bone structure that made him look famished, motioned to his son to sort out the pot, and came forward to greet the officers with great politeness, if not warmth. He had the air of a man lost in thought.

"Good morning to you, Mr. Eade. My name is Inspector Candy and this is DC Brady. We'd like you to answer some questions, if it's convenient."

"Jayne said the police called. Said it was about the girl that's gone missing." He spoke with a broad Norfolk accent, standing straight, unflinching beneath the harsh electric light and the razor sharp gaze of the inspector.

Alice Candy made no comment.

It was Will who spoke. "We're interested in the van outside. It was seen near the place Ellie Braintree may have disappeared, on the fourteenth of August." The police officer referred to his notes, pencil poised.

"Ah, I see." He looked at his son, as though for reassurance, then continued. "Well, we use the van for deliveries. But it's got a busted gearbox just now. Thinking of getting shot of it altogether, eh son? No idea about dates. Not good with that sort of thing any more." He tapped the side of his head and scowled.

"You'll have to ask Andy here, or Jayne. They'll know. Be sure to."

Giving his father an affectionate nod, Andrew Eade carried the tea tray to the table and sat down to pour.

"The fourteenth, you say? That was Mum's birthday. She didn't do the deliveries that morning. Ben did them in the afternoon."

The others took their places around the table.

"Well I never! You're right! Of course – her birthday! Your mum spent all day shopping, then went to the hairdresser's." Eade laughed, shaking his head. "Should have remembered that, eh? Bound to have cost me a pretty penny."

Andrew Eade smiled fondly at his father and handed round the tea, placing a milk jug and a sugar bowl in the centre of the table.

"Who is Ben, Mr. Eade?"

The older man seemed suddenly more lucid. "Young chap. Pleasant enough. Second time we've used him, I think. Our regular help's off on family business for a while, isn't that right, Andy? New chap's looking for regular work. Ben Benson – got his card somewhere, I think."

As his father finished, Andrew got up and went over to the sideboard. He opened a drawer and handed the card to Will Brady.

"And you say he took the yellow van that afternoon?" Alice Candy continued.

"That's it. He did. Pretty sure he did. When did he pick it up, Andy?"

"Around two. Brought it back around seven. Said something about having a flat."

Alice Candy stood up, leaving her tea untouched. "We'll need to check the van's interior, Mr. Eade. To your knowledge, has it been cleaned recently?"

"Cleaned?" Eade brought down his hand onto the table top, making the crockery clatter. His laugh was explosive. "More like sterilised! Jayne does it after every delivery. Bit of a love affair with the old soap and bleach, eh, son?"

"I heard that, Michael Eade!"

In the entrance to the kitchen, stood Jayne Eade, her eyes busy and her cheeks pink with curiosity.

Chapter Fifteen

Once again, Ellie had not heard the key turn in the lock after the door had closed, but, no matter how she jiggled the stick she'd found, the keyhole was too small to get the right angle. In the end, it snapped and fell onto the other side.

"Shit!"

"I told you it was a waste of time," said Donna.

"Do you think he'll notice it?"

"Doubt it. Too dark, and the floor's thick with dirt."

"Hmm." Ellie stayed crouched by the door, thinking.

"Come over here and tell me some more about you," said Donna, in the end.

Ellie had stood up then and come back to the bed, carrying the laden tray. It was no use. The door wouldn't budge. And there was nothing sturdier in the room she could use. What she needed was a piece of metal. A hanger. Something she could bend to reach the latch and push it up. In the meantime, looking at the tray and its contents, a thought struck her.

"Very strange." Ellie set it down between them on the bed.

"What's strange?"

Ellie contemplated the contents of the tray a little longer. "Why is he making such an effort?"

"What? A pot of strawberry yoghurt, a bit of

crappy chicken salad and a can of Fanta? It's hardly a gourmet meal!"

"Yes, but it's kind of balanced, you know? And it *looks* nice."

"Maybe he doesn't want our hair to fall out. Maybe he's a bloody chef in training! Who knows?"

"No, I think he's trying to please us."

"Please us? What the hell are you talking about? He's locked us up in a cellar!"

"I think he's sorry for us. Donna, do you think there's someone else in the house? Someone telling him what to do? Maybe he's a prisoner too. Maybe he doesn't have any choice but to bring us food and wash our clothes, empty our bucket."

"Why would you think that? You have an over-active imagination, Ellie, you know that?"

The girls ate. But Ellie had an idea going round and round in her head. Something wasn't right. In the silence of the room the sound of their chewing was oddly functional. Soulless. It was unsettling to be eating the food that had been prepared for them by a person who kept them under lock and key, who never spoke, who never made any demands of them.

"How long do you think you've been here?" asked Donna.

"You've already asked me that."

"Okay, how long do you think I've been here, then?"

"Two and a half days. Why?"

"Not bad. Two days, two hours and fifteen minutes."

Ellie stared. "You have a watch!"

"So? What's the big deal?" Donna grinned.

"God, Donna! Let me see!"

It was Tuesday the twenty-third of August, at two

o'clock in the afternoon. Lunchtime.

"I've been here nine days!"

It was strangely comforting to be able to put an accurate figure to the time she had spent there. She'd been counting, but somehow *knowing* the date by looking at it on a proper timepiece was so much more reliable.

Her first thought was for her family. Nine days with their daughter missing was a terribly long time for her parents to cope with. Ellie could see them in her mind's eye, comforting each other, hoping for the best and fearing the worst. And Dom. Dom would never believe she were... he would never give up. The thought of all this and the fact that Donna was wearing a watch that could record the passing of each minute, hour and day, was suddenly overwhelming and, in spite of herself, she could not hold back the tears that came silently, falling onto her plate. The sight of the perfect, red tomatoes and the jolly yoghurt pot increased her distress. Nothing made sense. It always came back to that. She needed to find out what was going on. She had to work it out or she would go mad.

"Come here," said Donna, putting the tray aside and holding Ellie close.

"I'm all right! Just leave me."

"Yes, I know. But just relax. I'm here now. Don't be scared."

Then it came to her. And all the little pieces that had not fitted, began to slot into place to give her a picture. It wasn't a completed picture, but it was a beginning. With her head resting on Donna's chest, she felt the shape of the girl's jaw and the hardness of her chin against the back of her head. Looking down, she saw arms wrapped around her and felt hands clasping her. It was all she could do not to break free and accuse Donna there and then, but Ellie knew she should take time to reflect. Appalled as she was by the ideas going round in her head, it would be imperative to keep them to herself for the time being, imperative not to let Donna see. She didn't know whether she could do it. She didn't know whether Donna had already guessed that she suspected something. Her body might have given her away, her unwillingness to yield to Donna's embrace might seem odd. And so, to give herself time to control her emotions, she forced herself to relax, letting the heat in her body, which was now nothing to do with despair, pass out of her. Her mind raced, going over the details, making sure that she was not mistaken. Small comments, tiny slips.

"Poor Ellie. You've been so strong. Don't worry. I'm telling you, we're going to be fine. Just fine. Trust me."

Chapter Sixteen

"Pete? Is that you Pete?"

There was a lot of background noise. The sound of traffic. And then, nothing.

"We know it was late evening. It wasn't rush hour. But it was busy. There was substantial traffic pulling out, moving slowly. So, he was close to a main road. The data shows that engine noise is not constant. There's gear shifting. It's likely that there's a crossing or traffic lights nearby." Jerome Blaize was not particularly surprised at the banality of the information he'd gathered from the recording. But finding a name, now that was something.

"He wasn't driving?" asked Alice Candy.

"No. If he'd been driving, we would be able to pick up a higher decibel reading from his engine. It would be greater than the background noise. No, the cars are passing him by, in both directions."

"Why is the man's voice so muffled? It sounds as though it's coming from a distance. We couldn't hear anything clearly on the phone itself."

"Aha. Well there are several possible explanations, but the most likely is that he was not familiar with the phone and was either holding it wrongly, or had placed a hand over the microphone."

Alice Candy considered the implications of Jerome's words and the dancing light in his eyes, which contradicted the deadpan expression on his face.

"What kind of person would not know how to speak into a mobile phone?"

Jerome was a professional, but he also drew on intuition. "It could have been picked up by kids. Testing it out between themselves."

"No, children wouldn't sound so serious. And what child would not know how to use such a device?' Inspector Candy paused. "Is it possible that the speaker was holding something over his mouth?"

"If he were, we'd be able to detect a level of distortion in his voice associated with muffling."

Alice Candy considered the evidence so far, then asked, 'Haven't you got equipment to give us a voice profile?"

"Already done. It's not altogether reliable. The parameters are consistent with a speaker of between sixteen and twenty-five. His voice has broken, but the timbre is weak. Could just be a lack of confidence. This is conjecture, of course. The sample isn't very comprehensive."

"So it could be a teenager, or a young adult?"

"Most likely."

"And your personal opinion, Jerome?"

"I'd bet my last ten that it's a young man, in his late teens to early twenties, with some kind of learning difficulty. Call it a gut feeling."

Jerome's gut feelings were rarely wrong. He knew it, and Alice Candy knew it too. They listened again. The words were tentative, that much was obvious. As though the speaker already knew that it was not Pete on the line, that checking was futile, even dangerous. Alice Candy pictured him walking along a busy road, startled by the ringing of the stolen phone in his pocket, fumbling as he answered, and hanging up when he realised his error.

"The phone was switched on. Can you tell for how long?"

"No. Only real time measurements can be made."

"Can you trace it?" Alice knew what the answer would be, but she had to ask.

"Nope. If it's not switched on, we can't. We checked to see whether the girl had installed the 'find my phone' app. But she hasn't. No GPS, no chance. Even with it, the trace is not accurate enough to be of much use. Maybe NASA might do better, but I doubt it."

"How about setting an alert for when it's switched on again?"

"Good idea. We're working on it."

They both knew that the likelihood of that happening was close to zero.

In the meantime, a search for all men between fifteen and forty with Peter as a first name, living in the immediate vicinity was ongoing. There would be hundreds. Alice Candy had faith in her team. She had to have faith.

*****

Ben Benson had been located and was downstairs in the interview room. The inspector was anxious to get hold of the interview transcript, so she hung around outside the windowless door, wishing she had a two-way mirror to observe him through. No budget. No mirror.

"How long's he been in there, Steve?"

The duty officer looked up from his paperwork and frowned, consulting the clock opposite his desk. "More than half an hour, now."

And, just at that moment, DC Brady emerged, closing the door quietly behind him.

He passed the statement to Alice Candy and together they took the stairs to her office.

"Did you ask him to stay?"

"Yes. He wasn't too pleased."

Once seated at her desk, Alice put her head down and Will didn't speak for the next five minutes.

"What do you think of his story?" asked the inspector, turning back to the beginning.

"Sounds viable to me, but there's a lot we can look into."

"Did you check with the Eades that they were expecting him to pick up from Henry Downs' allotment?"

"Not yet, couldn't get hold of them. But I had someone telephone Henry Downs during the interview. He confirmed that there were seven bags of new potatoes, best quality and last of the season, waiting for collection."

"Do the times check out? Benson says he took the van back at seven pm. Says he had a flat."

Will checked his notes taken during the initial visit to the Eades' farm. "All the tyres on the van have repairs to them. The spare has a flat. Looked as though it could have been sliced."

"On purpose?"

"Would seem that way."

Inspector Candy paused. When she looked back to Will, she realised that he was considering her new hair style. She'd had the fringe cut back so that it no longer fell forward.

"Like it?"

"It makes you look…younger."

"You don't say?"

A twinkle passed between them.

"So, a sliced spare. Still, over two hours late. How long does it take to change a wheel?"

"About ten minutes, if you know what you're doing. Do you want me to look into it further, Boss?"

"With the eye of a hawk! Run a check on the deliveries list. Double-check delivery times, especially the last one. The sighting of the van, according to the Werrels, was just before the number eight bus pulled up at four-thirty. Presumably, Benson would have scheduled the potatoes pick up for when he'd finished his round. So, between four-thirty and seven, what was he up to?"

"Says he was running late."

"Get back to me today, Will. And book Benson in for a second interview in the next twenty-four hours. I want to ask him a few questions of my own."

Chapter Seventeen

When Ellie woke up, she felt groggy and she had a headache. It was as though a lead weight were pressing down on the top of her head and she groaned, turning over and bringing her knees up under the blanket. Her eyes blinked open as she gained consciousness. Soon, staring into the darkness, she had the strange feeling that something or someone had disturbed her sleep. There was no glimmer of light. Not from the ceiling. Not from the lamp. As her thoughts became clearer Ellie knew that, in the darkness, something had changed once more. All at once, she felt a vacuum. The space next to her in the bed was empty.

"Donna?"

There was no reply.

"Donna, are you there?"

Ellie sat up and fumbled for the lamp. It was not in its usual place under the bed. That's when the panic rose inside her, just as it had on the day she'd woken up alone and bound by the wrists with tape over her mouth. This time, she controlled it.

Breathe. Listen.

All she could hear for the next few seconds was the throbbing of her own heart beat drumming in her ears. She waited, stunned in the silence. Nothing. And no one.

The door lay before her, barely visible, closed and locked as usual no doubt. She got out of bed and tried it, anyway. No good. And then the questions started. Where was Donna? When had he taken her? Why? Her thoughts of Donna's complicity suddenly seemed ridiculous. Shameful. How could she be involved? But, it had been such a strong feeling. Like an intuition. And there were other, more tangible clues. Things she'd said sometimes, as though she knew more than she should. She knew what was on the other side of the door, she knew that the man would not see the broken stick in the dirt, she knew that everything would be all right. And her version of the attack. It had just sounded made up. Asking someone for directions and then being forced into the back of his van. Why would the man have got down from his cab? And where did all this happen? Ellie realised that she didn't even know what time of day it had been, or the name of the town or village where it had happened. And the watch? Ellie was certain that Donna had teased her with it. There were too many inconsistencies. She had to be in on it. Didn't she?

And now she'd vanished.

Ellie's headache wore off a little after she'd drunk two large cups of water and gone back to lie down with the blanket wrapped around her, waiting for the soft glimmer of daylight to arrive. Standing up had been an effort. Walking unsteadily, her limbs heavy, she'd held on to the wall to keep her balance.

Some time later, the tray slid in, and she made a

rush for the door. This time she got her fingertips round it, but the grip was weak and with one good yank from the other side, she let go rather than get her fingers trapped.

"What have you done with Donna?" she shouted. "Don't hurt her! Do you hear me? Leave her alone!"

After all her logically worked out conclusions, Ellie knew that there was always a margin for error. If Donna really had been taken, she wanted to be sure that she'd done her best to protest on her behalf. If Donna had been taken, it would be her turn next! She drummed on the door with her fists and shouted:

"DON'T TOUCH HER! D'YOU HEAR ME!"

She was certain that whoever was on the other side of the door had waited longer than usual. Only now did the key turn in the lock, and Ellie ducked to look through the keyhole. In the distance was a dim light, but there was nothing to see of the figure that must be receding. Only just before the light disappeared did she glimpse a human shadow. The same as she'd seen on several occasions, a fuzzy outline of indeterminate size. A ghost. A phantom. A monster.

Ellie trembled with frustration. With fury. Now there was no lamp! How on earth had he managed to take Donna and remove the lamp from under the bed? She was not a heavy sleeper. Had he drugged the food last night? That would have made it easy for him to sneak in and carry Donna away without a fight. He would have to be strong and dextrous to lift her and take the lamp at the same time. Ellie's head still ached, although the awful throbbing had subsided. Yes. That must be it. The food had been drugged.

Food. Ellie sniffed the air. For the first time, apart from the burger, there was the smell of hot food. She collected the tray and put it next to her on the bed. There was pasta with what looked like chicken. And, if she was not mistaken, there was oregano and black pepper. Was it lunchtime already? She felt confused, unable to remember the previous few hours. The food looked good. But could she eat it? In the end, she decided that this meal would be safe. If he'd wanted to take her, he would have done it during the night. The truth was, that Ellie was very hungry and the lure of a proper cooked meal was too much to resist.

The food tasted homemade. There was ice cream, too. Ben and Jerry's. Cookie Dough. For some reason, it nearly made her laugh. But Ellie ate the meal and was thankful for it. Could Donna have prepared it? She imagined Donna and whoever else was upstairs, sitting on a comfortable sofa, perhaps watching a film together and enjoying a glass of wine. Just as she and Dom would be doing if she were not locked away in a cellar, alone and in the dark.

Without the lamp, she could not read, she could not write, but she had her thoughts, her memories. She would not be broken. Ellie could conjure music, a special memory, snippets of conversation. She saw Dom and Paul arm wrestling, making ridiculous faces. She saw her old school friend Sam gazing stupidly at their Biology teacher, missing the fact that he'd just asked her a question. She saw her mum coming up behind her in the mirror, telling her how beautiful she was.

She didn't want to feel alone, now that Donna had gone, and so in the relative darkness, she began to sing. Faintly, at first, a song her mother used to listen to called 'I Will Survive!' A song she didn't particularly like, but whose words she knew by heart. She stood up and started to dance, singing more and more loudly, turning round and round, throwing her arms up and jumping. Unafraid to move freely, in a space she knew by instinct. It made her feel good. Strong. When the song was finished, she started another. If she didn't know the words, she made them up. It was wonderful. Magic. In her mind, there was the sky above and the green grass below. There were clouds rushing by, multi coloured and lit by golden sunlight. There were people watching, laughing, joining in. Faster and faster she danced, filling the space with her turning and jumping, filling the emptiness with her voice, so clear. Like a bell ringing out. Ellie didn't want to stop. It felt good to be alive, even here. Even here.

Finally, she threw herself down onto the bed, exhausted and, perhaps for the first time since she'd arrived, glowing with heat and courage, she believed she would outwit her captor and get out of the cellar. She was agile, strong and determined. She would survive.

After her exertions, the rest of the day passed slowly, but Ellie overcame the temptation to remain on the bed and doze, so she walked. When she was bored with walking, she skipped, when she was tired, she stretched. All the time, she considered her options, and tried not to imagine what might be happening to Donna. The evening meal arrived, and this she did not eat, but kept in a napkin, hidden from sight. If he came for her, she would not be unconscious. She would pretend to be drugged, allow him to carry her in his arms and, at an opportune moment, make her escape. This was the thought she held fast in her mind. Escape.

Sleep came quickly when she finally climbed into bed. The exercise had tired her.

When Donna crawled back in next to her, Ellie awoke and let out a scream. The girl was wet, from head to foot, and shivering violently.

"Donna? Oh! What's wrong? What's happened?"

"He... he took me, Ellie."

Ellie sat up, wishing she had a light.

"You're soaking! Here, put the blanket round you. What happened, Donna? Why are you wet?" It was a strange question to ask, Ellie knew but her brain sought an explanation and she was still not fully awake.

Donna simply repeated the same thing, over and over again. "He took me, Ellie. He took me!"

Ellie made her get up and undress. Then, she rubbed her down with one of the towels and dressed her in a set of spare clothes and a dressing gown on top. She took off her own socks, as there were no others, and put them on Donna's feet. Even then, the girl was still numb, her teeth chattering uncontrollably.

It was no good trying to get anything out of her and so Ellie wrapped her up as best she could and held her close for what seemed like hours, until Donna stopped shivering and fell asleep.

Ellie too must have slept, for it was Donna who woke her.

"Ellie?"

She opened her eyes and made out the shape of Donna's face close to hers.

"Thank you." Donna's words struck Ellie like a

hammer in her chest.

The girls stayed put. Not speaking much. Holding each other. When a tray arrived, Ellie carried it over, putting on the lamp that had been returned at the same time. When she did, she saw a bruise the size of a fist around Donna's left eye, and a small cut just under her nose.

"Jesus, Donna!"

"He hurt me, Ellie. I was so scared!"

Ellie stared. How could she have been so wrong? The poor girl had been attacked, no doubt about it.

"Did he…?"

"No. No, not that. Not that."

Anger rose in Ellie. "What happened, Donna? You have to tell me everything. We have to get out of here. What did you see up there? We have to get out before…" She wanted to say, *before this happens again*, but Donna smiled and said, "Don't worry, Ellie. I won't let him hurt you. You are too precious. You are my friend."

The same smile came again. The smile that was so wrong in the circumstances. "Let's eat," Donna said, sitting up and swinging her legs over the side of the bed. "We have to keep our strength up."

Ellie put the tray between them and watched Donna bite into a sandwich.

"It's good. Eat. We have to eat." Donna spoke with her mouth full.

Ellie picked up a sandwich, sniffed it and opened it up to look inside. Then she put it to her lips.

Chapter Eighteen

"What's for breakfast, then, Joe? Got any bacon, eggs?"

After Joe's most recent shopping trip the fridge was well stocked. "There's lots of bacon, and there are six brown eggs and two creamy ones."

"Yeah? Creamy eggs? Sounds good to me."

Joe grinned at Pete.

Pete stared back at him, eventually saying, "Get going, then! Stick the kettle on. You got real coffee? That stuff we had last night was poison. And, what's with the temperature? Open the door – it's like a furnace in here."

Joe did as he was asked, then ducked down to pull out a frying pan from a cupboard under the hob. He set it down carefully, and went to the fridge to find the rashers he'd bought at the supermarket. Streaky bacon. Smoked. Ten rashers for ninety-nine pence.

The kettle boiled quickly. Joe was washing out the coffee pot.

"What're you doing? The pot's clean."

Joe looked around, set the pot down and handled the instant coffee jar, not opening it.

Pete was staring again. He spoke slowly. "Do you know where the proper ground coffee is?" Then, under his breath, "Christ, can't you listen?"

"Sorry, Pete."

Joe put down the coffee jar and went out of the room. He came back with a packet of Lavazza.

Pete was out of his chair, stretching his arms to the ceiling. He brought them down with a deep yawn and said, "Great stuff! See? I knew I could count on you! That'll put hairs on your chest." He grinned widely and slapped Joe on the back.

Joe laughed nervously. Pete was strong. Pete was clever. He knew what to do. But, last night, while Joe had been getting Ellie's tray ready, Pete had been angry. Joe remembered the beer bottle he'd thrown. The bits of glass had gone everywhere. Donna had shouted and Pete had shouted back, putting his face close to hers and holding her by the shoulders. Joe hadn't liked that. But Donna had given him a look that said, *stay back, Joe. I can handle this.* Pete had let her go then and told Joe to clear up the fucking mess. When Pete swore, it was frightening.

Joe had looked at Donna again. "Go on, Joe. It's okay," she'd said. So Joe had swept up the glass and put it in the bin.

Pete had opened another beer and sat down at the table, scraping the chair noisily. Then things had quietened down for a while. Donna had prepared a hot meal for Ellie. It looked and smelled delicious.

But more trouble came when Joe opened the door to the passageway that led to the cellar. He held the tray of food, reading the words on the ice cream tub. Then something caught his attention. There was the sound of singing.

Pete had laughed, his face dark with violence, and said he would go and give Ellie something to sing about. Donna had tried to stop him, but Pete had caught her by the wrists and called her names like *twisted* and *cracked*. Pete had laughed at Donna then, but not in a friendly way.

"Just take the tray, Joe," his sister had said, calmly.

Pete had grinned, mimicking her. "Yeah, take the tray, Joe. There's a good boy."

Joe had done as he was told, despite the feelings that threatened to burst out of him. Donna knew best. He must do as she said.

When he'd come back, Donna had told him to eat his meal in the lounge – she and Pete had things to talk about. He'd turned on the television but his mind still dwelled on what Pete had said. Joe knew what 'twisted' meant, but not the way Pete used it, not to describe a person. He knew better what 'cracked' meant: It could mean that something was damaged or almost broken, *including* a person. At school, it had been one of the names the other children had used to hurt him. *Cracked, mental, stupid, retarded...* so many names, rattling out like bullets from a machine gun. Like the machine gun on the television in front of him.

The sound from the television had not blocked out the noise from the kitchen. Donna was shouting. There was the sound of crashing furniture. Joe put his hands over his ears. There it was, still! He couldn't bear it and, finally, he'd switched off the film and gone outside with Jess to look at the stars. Outside, there was only the sound of the wind and the rattling of the barn doors.

That had been last night. Now, Pete was different. He whistled and got up to pour the boiling water onto the coffee. The other, violent Pete seemed less real.

The smell of coffee was nice. But the taste was bitter. Joe didn't like the bitterness, so he added sugar. Lots of sugar. *Sugar's not good for you, Joe,* his mother always said. Joe missed his mother. He wished that she would come back soon.

"What's up, Joe? Don't you worry, eh? Eh, Joe? Everything'll work out fine, you'll see. As long as you keep shtum, eh?" Pete moved his fingers across his lips. "Keep it zipped, eh Joe?"

Don't say a word, Joe.

Joe sipped his coffee and looked at Pete. His hair was untidy and he was wearing the same clothes he'd had on the night before. There were puffy bags under his eyes. Pete looked tired.

Joe ventured a question – he hadn't seen his sister since the previous night. "Pete? Did Donna go to see Ellie?"

Pete stirred his coffee and stared at Joe, a thin smile twitching his top lip. "Sure did, Joe. Last night. Way before you poked your nose out of bed this morning."

Joe had been up before Pete. So how would he know when he'd poked his nose out of bed? After a moment, he said, "I took breakfast - enough for two. I didn't know, so I took enough for two people. For Ellie and Donna. And I took the lamp. They..."

Pete lowered his raised cup. He spoke quietly. Too quietly. Joe knew he had done something wrong and his legs suddenly felt weak.

"You took the fucking lamp?" Pete shook his head, clicked his tongue. His voice rose with each word he spoke. "Why did you go and take the *fucking* lamp, Joe? *Chrissake!*" Pete slammed his coffee cup onto the table and it splashed messily, making a puddle inside the butter dish. Jessie started and slunk over to Joe.

Joe didn't want to look at Pete. He picked Jess up,

stroking her gently, and sought to explain himself very carefully. "Ellie likes the lamp. She wrote for it the first time."

"*Christ!*" Pete pushed back the chair, stood up and took out a cigarette, leaning forward, tapping it on the table close to Joe. Tapping it too many times. Joe caught the smell of his stale shirt and the scent of coffee and cigarettes.

"Did I make a mistake, Pete?"

"*Did I make a mistake, Pete?*" His voice was sing-song.

Joe bent his head forward and stared at his shoes. His pants felt baggy under his trousers. His skin prickled with shame and he wanted to get away. To get away for good. Jess was still in his arms, and Joe gave her a look. The same kind of look that Donna gave him when there was trouble, *Everything's okay, Jess. Don't worry*.

Pete stood back a little and laughed. He lit his cigarette and threw the match down. He stared right at Joe, watching him petting Jess. Joe knew he was staring. He could sense it.

In the end, Pete sat down again and spat out words that broke the tension. "Leave that stupid dog alone and finish my breakfast. D'you think you can you do that without mucking it up?"

Joe didn't like Pete calling Jess stupid, but he knew better than to say anything. He set her down and told her to lie in her basket, his voice gentle.

Pete was not his friend. Pete didn't like Jess. Anyone who was unkind to Jess could never be Joe's friend. Never.

Joe turned his back on Pete and soon got the bacon sizzling. He cracked in the eggs, just as his mother had taught him how to, and sliced bread thickly to make toast. He warmed the plate in the microwave. When everything was ready, Joe laid out a tray, just as he did for the girls who were staying in the cellar room, and put it down carefully in front of Pete, who was now reading the newspaper.

Pete folded the paper and pulled the tray towards him. "Your sister is a first class bitch, you know that?"

Joe felt a tightening in his chest, as though it were being held in a vice. He imagined tipping the tray up onto Pete's lap, pouring the hot coffee over his head.

Cutting into the toast and dipping it into the egg, Pete wasn't finished. "She's not right in the fucking head, either. Must run in the family, eh? Eh, Joe?"

Joe didn't want to listen to Pete. Donna always said that if you didn't want to listen to someone who was being rude to you, you could think about something nice instead. Now, Joe thought about a day he had spent at the beach, years ago. The smallest waves running up towards him, rippling over his toes. His sister wading in deep to fill her bucket, unafraid. There had been sunshine and ice creams, shells with smooth insides and rough ridges on the outside, seagulls flying in circles, people running, children laughing. The beach was a happy place. And safe. As long as Donna were nearby.

"Got any ketchup?" Pete asked.

Joe put the bottle on the table.

"You not having any breakfast?" Pete was reading the paper again.

"I'm not hungry," replied Joe.

Pete grunted, without looking up.

Joe sat on a chair next to Jessie's basket.

It had been nice to see his sister when she came out of the cellar. She'd kissed him and said he'd done really well. Ellie was happy, she said, and loved the beautiful trays he put together. If he carried on in the same way, everything would be fine. Joe had asked her why, if Ellie was so happy, did she run at the door and try to get out. Why did she shout and say things like: *don't hurt her!* Donna had put her arms around him and explained that friendship could be up and down, and that Ellie needed time to settle in, to feel safe. The cellar was a safe place. Nothing bad could happen in the cellar. Then, with Pete standing there, listening, she'd whispered in his ear – the same thing she'd said from the start: *You needn't worry, Joe. I'll make everything right, okay?* Her breath tickled and he couldn't keep the smile from his face. The smile that Pete said made him look like even more of an idiot than he really was.

Later, when they had been alone for a moment, Donna had stood right in front of him and looked straight into his face when she spoke: *This is important, Joe. If the police come and find you. If things go bad. Don't say a word. You hear me? They won't understand what we're trying to do. Even if they take me away and say I'm locked up in prison and you are the only one who can get me out. It's not true, okay? It's not true, Joe. They'll just try to trick you. So they can make you talk. So don't talk, Joe. Okay? Don't say a word.*

As she'd continued to speak, Joe had concentrated hard. He'd listened to the words as Donna slotted them one by one into his brain. The thought that something might go bad terrified him. He didn't understand what this meant. And the police. Why would they find him? What had he done wrong?

What had Donna done wrong?

As his mind raced, he'd felt his stomach tighten and his breathing quicken. Then there was Donna's face, close to his, again. Looking at him hard and saying: *So don't talk, Joe. Okay? Don't say a word.*

When Pete had come back, he'd told Joe to get lost. As Joe had passed by, he'd deliberately pushed into Pete's shoulder. Pete had laughed. But Joe didn't feel like laughing at all. He was thinking about the beach again. This time about a crab that he'd found in a rock pool. Donna had said it was dirty. A dirty creature. She had raised her spade and brought it down, once, twice, three times. When the water had cleared, the crab was nowhere to be found. And Joe was crying. Pete was a dirty creature. Much dirtier than the crab.

It hadn't been long before Donna and Pete had gone upstairs together. That was after the fight. And Joe had got to thinking, not for the first time, about why Donna spent so much time with Pete. She didn't seem to like him much. She liked Ellie much better. Pete was mean to her. Ellie was her friend. Donna had brought Ellie to stay because she wanted to save her. Donna was good at saving people. She had saved him. He knew. The crab had been a dirty creature and she had saved him from it. That was the first time he could recall how she had comforted him and told him everything would be all right.

What was going through his mind now, this morning, as Pete ate the breakfast he had prepared, was that it was his turn to save Donna. To save Donna from Pete.

"Not bad!" Pete pushed his plate away, belched, and put his feet up on one of the other chairs. He nodded at the coffee pot and Joe brought it to him.

"You should get out of here, you know. Get away from her. Get a job and find a nice flat in town. Christ! How old are you? Nineteen? Twenty?"

"I'm twenty-one in November."

"Twenty-one. If I were twenty one I'd sure as hell not be rotting in this place."

Joe cleared away the breakfast things and made a shopping list. Donna and Ellie would have a special lunch today. Pete could go to hell.

Chapter Nineteen

Ellie couldn't sleep. After Donna's ordeal, it was only logical that it would be her turn before long. She still had no idea what had happened. None. Donna wouldn't say much. Maybe she would feel able to open up a bit once she was more settled.

They'd eaten well, even talked. Donna was strangely cheerful, but prone to sudden fits of despair. She'd wanted to rest, asking Ellie to keep her warm. Ellie sighed and turned over, trying to get comfortable, hoping that her mind would calm so that she could sleep.

Just then, she felt something hard digging into her arm. There was something inside Donna's dressing gown pocket. Ellie slipped her hand carefully inside. Donna moaned in her sleep, but didn't wake up. There were shadows on the ceiling that made Ellie blink a little. The girls had slept with the lamp on under the bed. It was Ellie who'd insisted on this. Donna hadn't put up much of a fight. But the shadows tonight made Ellie more fearful than usual.

Clasping the object inside Donna's pocket, she drew out a small bottle. How had it got there? It hadn't been there when she'd given the dressing gown to Donna. Curious to see what was inside, Ellie brought it nearer to her face then leaned over the side of the bed, bringing it into the light, moving gently. It was a bottle of pills. The label bore the name of Amanda Leighton. Amanda Leighton? It was a name she knew, but she couldn't place it. On the second line, she read *rohypnol*. And on the line below that, *take one to two tablets, as required*. She turned the bottle around. There were more than a few tablets inside. Pushing the bottle inside the pocket of her gown, she sat up carefully, wide awake.

Donna stirred. "Ellie?"

"It's okay, Donna. I'm just getting a drink. Go back to sleep."

Amanda Leighton. Amanda Leighton. Could it be? Amanda Leighton, St. Charlotte's junior school. There'd been a girl called Mandy. Yes. Mandy Leighton. Ellie saw her now, medium height, with mousy hair, an almost perfectly round face, and a weight problem. She'd been the class busybody too. Always telling tales and cosying up, first to one person, then another. Could it really be her?

Donna was sleeping soundly once more. Ellie pulled the lamp out from under the bed and increased its brightness. Donna's hair was blond, but the roots were coming through, mousy roots. Her face was not as round, but it did lack definition. She was definitely not overweight, if anything, Ellie had thought her too thin. Mandy. Mandy the Meddler. *Here she comes. Quick, scram!*

In the last term, it had been Ellie's turn to be chosen. Her friends had said she should tell Mandy straight. *Tell her she's not wanted. Tell her nobody wants to know a sneak.* But Ellie had not. She'd spent time with Mandy. Lots of time. The girl was not so bad. Just a little too clingy, a little too overbearing. Eventually, the end of year exams had come and they had gone their separate ways. Ellie had not kept in touch with her.

Could this be the same girl? Mandy Leighton had

gone off to train as a secretary. That's all she knew. And then, all at once, Ellie recalled a detail: a pink scar on her wrist, about two inches long and slightly curved at one end. Mandy had slipped and cut herself on a sharp stone in the playground. There had been blood. Lots of blood. Mandy had shown Ellie the stitches, which had looked like insect's legs sticking out of her flesh. The scar had earned Mandy a little kudos – everyone wanted to see it. Which wrist had it been? The left one. Slowly, Ellie turned. Donna's left arm lay on top of the blanket. There was her watch, with its black leather strap. Holding her breath now, Ellie brought the light nearer. Was it her imagination? Had the cellar made her paranoid? The black strap was wide, covering the place where the scar would be. Ellie squinted. Was there something? Maybe. Yes! There was a small, livid curve just a few millimetres long, sticking out from underneath the strap. Ellie stared, then looked once more at Donna's face. Mandy Leighton. Amanda Leighton. Suddenly, things began to make sense!

It took very little time for three tablets to dissolve in the glass of water. Ellie added some of the orange juice from the cartons they'd had with their last meal. Soon the door would be opened and dinner would be delivered. She must hurry. Ellie stirred the drink and took a sip - it was strangely sweet with a bitter after taste. She added more juice.

Donna woke when Ellie sat down on the bed again. "Uh? What time is it?"

"You're the one with the watch, silly," Ellie laughed.

Donna sat up, ruffling her hair and grinning. "What've you got?"

"Just some orange mixed with water." Ellie took a sip. "Want some?"

"Please. Mmm. I'm thirsty just watching you."

"Here. You have this one, I'll make another."

"Thanks, Ellie. I knew I wasn't wrong about you. You're a good person, you know."

"I do my best!" She felt the heat rising in her cheeks. This girl was unbelievable!

Ellie went over to the sink and ran more water into another glass. Her heart felt as though it might burst out of her chest. It was all she could do to stop her hands from shaking. *I'm doing the right thing. I have to get out of here*. As calmly as she could, she added the last of the juice and went back to see Donna tipping her head back to finish her drink.

"Just what the doctor ordered."

Ellie's stomach jolted and her smile slipped.

Donna didn't notice. She seemed to be in good spirits and said, "It's coming up for seven. He'll be bringing dinner soon. D'you want me to read some of that new book to you? It looks okay. Here, sit next to me and we'll wrap the blanket around our legs."

Donna began to read. She had a good voice. But the more Ellie listened, the more she caught the twang of Mandy the Meddler's whingeing tones. And every now and then, she glanced at the telltale scar, almost concealed, but visible if you knew what you were looking for.

Ellie had no idea how long the drug would take to have an effect. She'd heard horrific stories about it, of course. It made you drowsy and brought on amnesia. She watched Donna for signs.

"Hey! Stop staring. People will talk!"

"Sorry." Ellie returned Donna's grin as naturally as

she could.

Donna put the book down for a moment. "I hope we can stay friends when we get out of this place."

Ellie couldn't reply. She felt as though her throat were being constricted. Luckily, it seemed that Donna thought her new friend overcome with emotion. Taking Ellie's hand, Donna spoke with new enthusiasm. "Listen, Ellie, I think I've got a plan... I've got some pills. We can pretend to take them and when he comes, we'll say we've taken an overdose and shove the empty bottle out for him to see. It'll fit under the door, easily. He'll panic. I know he will. Then, he'll open up."

Ellie froze. Her eyes would give her away. She must speak, say something to stop Donna reaching for the bottle.

"Look," said Donna.

Oh, no! Do something!

Ellie grabbed Donna's hand and raised it to her lips. She trembled as she spoke. "I'm so glad we had this time together, Donna. When I was here alone, I was so frightened."

Donna smiled and Ellie winced.

Again, Donna misread her reaction. "I know. But everything will be fine, you'll see. I'll look after you, Ellie."

At that moment, Donna fell forward and almost rolled onto the floor.

"Donna!"

Donna laughed and sat up again. "I'm so happy, Ellie!"

"Are you okay?"

"Yes. I mean, I *do* feel a bit strange..." Donna let go of Ellie's hand and felt inside her pocket. Her face contorted in disbelief. "No! What have you done,

Ellie?"

Ellie jumped up and Donna tried to follow her, but her legs gave way and she fell heavily onto the ground. Ellie waited a few minutes then hoisted her up onto the bed. Donna babbled, occasionally lashing out. As the drug took her over, she lay, shifting very little, moaning gently. Ellie found whatever she could to stuff inside the blanket, and wrapped the pillow in a brown jumper. Then, she wrote a note: 'Please help! We don't feel well', pushed it under the door and extinguished the lamp.

It seemed to take forever, but eventually, she saw the edge of the note disappear and she knew that he was looking through the hole. From her vantage point, in the darkness, Ellie could make out two distinct shapes in the bed. They looked convincing enough to her. She held her breath, not moving a muscle, sitting to the side of the door, ready to pounce.

Just as she was sure he had become suspicious and walked away, she heard the key turn in the lock. She waited for it to open enough to dive at the gap. When she did, the man fell forward clumsily into the cellar, and scrambling to her feet she ran, not stopping to see whether he was still down, desperate to reach the door ahead before he caught up with her. The passageway was longer than she'd imagined, but the door at the end of it was open. Sitting on the step was a small dog with a ribbon in its fur. The sight was so unexpected that Ellie whooped, half crying out, half laughing. Jessie barked and danced in a circle, snapping at her heels as she jumped over her and tried to get her bearings. She was in a large kitchen. There were three doors. One of them, up three steps, was open, but led into what looked like the interior of the house, two others were closed. She grabbed the handle to the first one. It was locked. Trying not to panic, she went for the other one and felt it give. She pushed it open, gasping, bolting for freedom, and ran straight into the arms of Pete.

Joe had got to his feet and dusted himself off. He couldn't quite understand what had happened. The dinner tray lay upturned on the floor and there, in the bed, the girls still slept. When he approached, though, he discovered how he had been tricked. Ellie was not there. Only Donna. What should he do? Donna groaned. Was she ill? He took up the lamp and shone it into her face.

When he saw the bruise, he cried out. "Donna! Your face! Wake up!"

But she only smiled, her eyes closed, moaning gently.

"Donna!"

He must get help. Go back to the kitchen. Call for an ambulance. Nine, nine, nine. Ask for a doctor. That's it. That's it. His face was wet with tears and saliva. His nose was running. This was an important moment. A moment when he must get things right. To save his sister. He ran along the passageway, stumbling in his haste on the steps to the kitchen. What he saw when he staggered to his feet confused and alarmed him into silence.

"Look what I found, Joe. Did you let her out to play?"

Ellie and Pete were in the kitchen standing close, Pete's arm was around her waist and Ellie had a terrible expression on her face. She struggled, but Pete just laughed.

Joe's mouth flapped before he found the words he needed to speak. "I... I... Donna's sick. We have to get a doctor." He made a lunge for the phone.

"Hey! Hey, Joe. Calm down, boy. There's no need for that. No need to panic, eh?" Pete stood in his way.

"Let go of me!" shouted Ellie, trying to peel away the fingers that were gripping her so tightly.

"Leave Ellie alone!"

"Stay out of it, Joe." Pete's words were full of pent up aggression.

"Donna needs a doctor!" Joe made another attempt to grab the phone, pushing Pete away.

Ellie shouted for help, struggling harder.

Pete tightened his grip on Ellie. "Shut up, or I'll knock you out, I swear! And *you*, calm down, I said! Donna doesn't want the police involved, remember? If you call for a doctor, he'll tell the police. Do you want that to happen?"

Joe didn't want the police to come. He shook his head and looked at Ellie in desperation.

"Let's go and see Donna, shall we? Come on, Joe. She'll be okay. She's a big strong girl."

Joe led the way, with Pete keeping hold of Ellie, who still struggled but didn't speak.

Everything was going wrong. There would be trouble and it would be all Joe's fault. He'd made a big mistake. Donna would be angry with him.

Pete switched on the light in the passageway. When they got to the cellar, he switched the light on there too, at the switch positioned outside the door.

"Christ! What a dump!" said Pete, genuinely shocked by what he saw. "It's nothing like the palace Donna told me about. Said it was a spare room. Christ, Joe!"

Joe went straight to his sister. "Donna! Wake up, Donna!"

"Just leave it to me, Joe. Everything will be fine if we keep our heads." Keeping one arm around Ellie, Pete drew back the blanket, revealing the bruise on Donna's face and darted a look at Joe. Then, as though butter wouldn't melt in his mouth, he turned to Ellie and said, "Who's been a naughty girl, then?"

"Let me go! You can't keep me here!"

"Now, why should I do that, eh? Let's just find the rest of those lovely pills, shall we?"

Ellie struggled as Pete checked the pockets of her gown.

"Aha!"

Turning to Joe, he said, "Get some water, Joe."

Ellie threw her head back, striking Pete on his chin.

"Sit down and shut up!" He threw her onto the bed and she hit her head on the wall. "Listen to me. You are going to do exactly as I say." He shook three pills into his palm, then one more.

"You can't make me."

Pete grinned.

Joe handed him the water. He should do something. But what? This was bad.

Ellie knocked the water out of Pete's hand.

"Hey! Listen! It's all the same to me. I can lock you in here. Me, Joe and Donna can just disappear. Think about it. No one knows where you are. Or, you can take these, go off to La La Land and forget all about what's happened. I'll take you to a nice deserted place I know and let you go. When you come round, you might be lost, you might be scared. But you'll be alive. What do you say? Make up your mind, Ellie."

Ellie hesitated, but then she held out her hand.

Joe was relieved. He knew that Pete was still angry, even though he had spoken quietly. Joe watched as, one by one, Ellie put the pills into her mouth and drank from the cup he'd refilled. He hoped she knew that he would not harm her.

"What are you giving her?" he asked Pete.

"The same thing she gave your sister."

"You're not... You're not... killing her, are you Pete?"

"No, Joe. Not killing her. The pills are special medicine. They make you sleepy and when you wake up, you can't remember what happened to you. So Ellie won't be able to remember us."

Joe stared. "Will Donna remember us?"

"Course she will. She won't forget everything. Just the stuff that happens now. Don't worry, Joe. Leave it all to me, eh?"

"Are you Donna's brother, Joe?" asked Ellie, softly.

Joe looked at her pale, anguished face and nodded. He wanted to say sorry, but Pete was speaking to him again:

"Why don't you go and put the kettle on, Joe. It'll take a while for Ellie to fall into a nice, cosy sleep."

"Don't leave me with him, Joe." Ellie had the same strong confidence that Donna had. She was not afraid.

"Shut up, I said!" Pete moved towards Ellie, his arm raised.

"Don't touch her! I'm staying here," said Joe.

"Don't you trust me, Joe? Do you think I'll have some fun with her, eh?"

The two questions were confusing. The answers would be different.

119

"I'm staying."

Pete grinned darkly. "I'd say we have a bit of a dilemma here. There's me wanting a nice cup of coffee, and there's this fly in the ointment, so to speak." Pete looked at Ellie, then said, "I get irritated when I don't get what I want, don't I Joe? So, I've got a new idea. We'll all go together and come back for Donna when she wakes. Lead the way, Joe, Ellie's getting sleepy."

Chapter Twenty

Alice Candy was frustrated. She was sure that she was missing something. And she was equally sure that time was running out. When she thought about Ellie now, there was less detail. Just darkness. And the same stale smell of dank earth. She'd sensed violence during her last meditation. The prognosis was deteriorating, but she would not give up. With the Werrels' information, the investigation had gained momentum – she must move quickly now.

Will Brady's report on the leads he'd followed up, and Benson's statement had arrived promptly on her desk. Both were thorough. All the deliveries were made before four-thirty, the story about the flat tyre had checked out. The spare had a puncture, a huge slash of a puncture. Benson had covered his tracks clumsily, still leaving a significant block of time between the Werrel's reported sighting of the yellow van at the allotments and its arrival back at the Eades' farm. Benson was clever, but not as clever as he thought he was.

Will sat in a chair on the other side of her desk, ready to be of service. It was like being watched by a faithful hound. A very good-looking one. He had the collar of his jacket turned up and was wearing an expression that would make most women swoon. Alice knew he was simply concentrating. And she knew that when she was ready for him, he would sit up straighter in his chair and lean forward, his notebook at the ready. Three lines would appear on his forehead and his eyes would narrow.

Alice Candy looked into her colleague's eyes and watched Will go through the actions she'd seen a hundred times. "Did you speak to all the people who took delivery that afternoon?"

"Yes. Some of them weren't actually there when the van came by, though."

"Hmm. Which ones?"

"These three addresses." Will laid open his notebook in front of her, turning it round and indicating the relevant paragraph. "One of them arrived just as Benson was leaving. The other two were at work, so the boxes were left outside the door, which is normal practice, apparently." Will's writing was clear, his notes organised.

"And the remainder all spoke to Benson?"

"Yes. Some of them were surprised not to see Jayne Eade. But when Benson told them it was her birthday, they didn't ask questions."

The inspector nodded. Will was wearing a new coffee-coloured shirt, open at the neck. She paused, knowing that he had registered her look. "Nice shirt."

He grinned. "Thanks."

It was natural to switch back to business. They had worked together for over a year now. There was no need to explain the odd distraction.

"What did they say about him?"

Will took his notebook and sat further back in his chair, running his fingers through his hair. Once, twice. "Just that he was polite. Cheerful. That kind of thing. Tall, late twenties or thereabouts. Short untidy brown hair. Tattoo on his left forearm. A mermaid. Bit of a cliché. All checks out."

Alice Candy wondered whether that meant Will

did not approve of tattoos, or whether he had a more tasteful one on some part of his body.

"Are you all right, Boss?"

"Yes. Yes, I'm fine. So, you double checked the arrival time back at Eades'?"

"Yeah. Two independent witnesses: Andrew Eade and one of their workers, Pamela Caron."

Alice Candy wanted to listen to the interview with Benson, again. She wondered whether Will would prefer to go home and watch a film. Put his feet up with a beer and a pizza.

"Are you okay to stay a while?"

"Not a problem." Will sat back and closed his eyes to listen more intently.

Alice Candy selected 'play' and they listened to Will's voice, informative and level, going through the correct procedures before questioning Benson.

The interview was twenty-three minutes long, but Alice stopped the recording several times to check a detail or ask a question: How did Benson seem when he answered that? Did you notice any change in his body language? What was he doing with his hands? By the end of the interview, Will looked tired and a little bemused.

They had discovered precisely nothing. Alice Candy saw Will glance at the clock on the wall, then back to the paperwork on her desk. She had pulled out the statement made by Cedric Werrel. Will Brady folded his arms and observed the inspector as she read. The minutes passed. She flipped the paper over. There was nothing new.

"Is it all right if we listen to once more? Then I'll let you go."

"Anything you say, Boss."

Alice Candy watched Will, her eyes in soft focus, as Cedric Werrel's young voice filled the office space. She knew that he, like she, pictured the boy, sitting next to his mother, doing his best to please her. He was a confident, articulate child. A bit skinny, with one of those faces that looked older than it was. Cedric answered each question with precision. His mother interjected from time to time, at which point, Will was obliged to indicate who was speaking, as PW Maureen Widness had been in the room also.

Alice Candy's eyes were closed now, but she was as far from sleep as it was possible to be.

As the interview came to a close, Will asked Cedric one last question. "Did you see anyone get out of the van?"

Cedric was certain. The van had been partially hidden by the bushes. He couldn't be sure. "I didn't see them get out."

Mrs. Werrel cut in again. "He's a very observant boy. He might well want to go into police work one day, mightn't you, Cedric?"

Will indicated the time, and announced that the interview had ended.

Alice Candy picked up the statement again and turned to the second page.

"Will?"

"Yes, Boss."

"Play the last bit of the interview again. The last question."

They listened. Will didn't notice anything and shook his head.

"Once more," said Alice, handing him the paper statement and indicating the word that she had circled in black biro, which was at odds with the recording.

Will listened, screwing up his face.

"You hear it?"

He heard it. On the written statement, there was the word 'him', where Cedric had clearly spoken the word 'them'.

"Get Cedric on the phone. And call up Mr. Edwards, too."

Chapter Twenty-one

Pete hadn't meant to hit Donna the previous night but, when they'd gone upstairs to get away from Joe, Pete had told her about the police interview and she'd overreacted. Gone overboard, in fact. Pete had known that she would.

He'd sat on the bed and pointed out that it was obvious they were going to want to question him after some busybody had reported seeing the van. He'd told Donna not to worry. He'd had a legitimate reason for being at the allotments and he'd spun the police a yarn about a flat tyre, which they'd fallen for. No problem. He'd sliced the tyre. The van was clean. Jayne Eade had seen to that.

But Donna wouldn't give it up. She'd nagged him, asking over and over again whether he'd mentioned her. Of course, he hadn't. He wasn't a fool. Not like her brother, Joe. If there was a worry, it was about what Joe would do under pressure. Then Donna had leapt at him, screaming and lashing out, telling him to leave Joe out of it. In the end, he'd fought back.

To be honest, when he thought about the mess Donna had got him into, he wondered why he was still hanging around. Maybe they'd been together for too long. When they'd met, he'd found her exciting, different. Now, he realised that she was just plain deluded. And reckless. The thing with Ellie had been a bit of fun, until Donna had slipped a couple of rohypnol into her drink and made her swallow it as she came around from the chloroform. They'd left her in the back of the van and driven to the house, carried her in and stuck her in the kitchen.

"Now what?" he'd said.

"Help me tie her up. And tape her mouth."

"No way! You said you knew her. You said you wanted to get your own back. You didn't say it was serious shit. I'm taking the van back. You'd better sort out what you're going to do when she comes round. She's not going to be happy." Donna hadn't looked at him. He didn't care. She'd have to manage on her own.

Ellie had been headline news to begin with, but then the police had put their heads together, mostly chasing their tails, and things had gone quieter. Pete wasn't really worried. He'd covered his tracks. They had nothing on him, as long as they didn't know about Donna. The silly cow was a liability. And Joe would have to be kept quiet too.

He'd tried to convince Donna to let Ellie go at the beginning. But she hadn't wanted to listen... "Get her out of here, for God's sake. She thinks you're a victim, yeah? She doesn't know your real name, she doesn't know about Joe or me. Just slip her a couple of those pills and we'll dump her. She's seen nothing. She'll remember nothing."

"I'll let her go soon. We're friends. She likes me."

"Friends? Since when do friends kidnap each other? Seriously Donna, you need help."

That was all in the past. Perhaps there was a way out, now that he was in charge. Joe would do what he was told if it meant keeping Donna out of jail. Ellie wouldn't remember anything much when she came round. She had no idea where she was. No way of tracing anyone to the house. Hell, she could be hundreds of miles away from home for all she knew.

Now, here she was in the kitchen, slumped like a rag doll. The girl was spark out. Not a glimmer. He watched the movement of her eyes beneath her lids. Probably having some of the best dreams she'd ever had. He liked her face. He liked her legs. Beneath the robe, she was probably a stunner.

Joe lumbered around like a clumsy kid – brought coffee and sat down opposite Ellie. "Can I go and see Donna?"

Pete took a sip and raised his eyes to the ceiling. The boy was getting on his nerves. Best to keep him sweet. "Nice coffee, Joe. Excellent aroma."

But Joe looked glum and, not for the first time, Pete wanted to slap him. There he was, talking to that dumb dog again, petting it, and glancing up at Ellie every chance he got. Too scared to say what was on his mind. Too stupid.

Pete stood up, took another slug of coffee and directed his words like a laser beam. He knew how to get the moron's attention. Knew what tone to take. Leaning in, two fists on the table, he levelled his gaze, unflinching, and spoke in a monotone, seeing the fear mount in Joe's eyes.

"Right. Listen. This is what we're going to do. I'm going to take Ellie to a safe place, so that when she wakes up she can get herself to hospital. When she wakes up, she'll be fine, but she won't remember much about us and she won't know where you and Donna live."

Joe stared, his top lip moved, but he didn't speak.

"Understand?"

He forced out a response. "Yes, but…"

Pete didn't care about 'buts'. He raised a hand and said, "Just listen. You have to disappear for a few days. Get on a bus and go and see your auntie. The one in Brighton. While you're away, I'll stay with Donna and make sure she's okay. I'll clean up the place and, if any nosey parkers come by, I'll get rid of them. When the coast is clear, I'll call you. Take this." Pete handed him Donna's phone. "Go on. It's okay. You know how to use it, right?"

"Yes, but..."

Pete could see the pathetic excuse for a human being was on the verge of tears. He had to play his trump card with sensitivity. Placing a hand on the boy's shoulder, Pete eased into a softer tone of voice. He cared about Joe. He cared about Donna. Of course he did. "No buts, Joe. Donna's relying on you not to mess this up. In a few days it'll all be over."

Joe's eyes had grown as big as saucers.

"You mustn't tell anyone about Ellie, that's all. If you do, the police will come and take you and Donna away. Understand?"

Pete watched his words sinking in. The boy's lips moved. He seemed to be murmuring something under his breath.

Don't tell them anything, Joe. Don't say a word. Even if they say I'm locked up in prison. They'll try to trick you.

When he spoke, it was with conviction. "I understand, Pete. I won't tell anyone anything."

"Good man, Joe. I knew we could count on you. Now, if you want to go and say goodbye to your sister, you can. Just a minute..."

Pete went to the cupboard and took down a plastic tub of paracetamol. He popped the top, standing with his back to Joe.

Joe waited patiently.

Pete turned around and grinned widely. "If she's awake, give her three of these. They're painkillers. They'll make her feel better."

Joe took the tub and put it in his pocket.

Pete held out his hand again. Perhaps there was another way to play this... "Let me check the battery on Donna's phone. I'll put it on charge while you're down there."

Joe handed back the phone and Pete winked. "That's the way, Joe. Leave it to me, eh?"

"And you'll take care of Ellie?"

"I'll take good care of her, don't you worry. She won't know a thing when she wakes up. Not a thing."

*****

The passageway was dark, so Joe put on the light – it was okay to do that now. He didn't like to think of Donna all alone in the cellar. When she woke, she would be afraid. Sitting on the bed, he touched her arm and she moved, trying to sit up.

"It's Joe," he said. "Are you all right, Donna?"

Donna's eyes fluttered open for a moment and she scowled.

"My head!"

Joe took out the tub and shook three tablets onto his palm, but when he tried to give them to her, she knocked them out of his hand.

"You have to take these. They're for your headache." He read the label. "They're paracetamol."

"Joe?"

"Yes, it's me, Joe."

He got out three more pills and fetched some water. Donna was barely conscious. Then he had an idea. He pushed the pills inside one of the juice cartons, filled it with water and shook it before re-inserting the straw.

Donna stared up at Joe as she took most of the drink and settled back onto the bed. He stroked her face and hair and told her that he had to go away for a while. That Pete would look after her until the coast was clear. She didn't respond.

When Pete appeared in the doorway, Joe rose slowly, reluctant to leave his sister. Pete had a strange look on his face.

"Change of plan, Joe." Stepping back into the passageway and closing the door, Pete disappeared from view. Then, Joe heard the key turn in the lock.

*****

Pete went back to the kitchen and drank another coffee, considering his options. This whole situation had been none of his making, so why shouldn't he just walk away? In the end, though, he carried Ellie outside and manoeuvred her onto the back seat of his car. If he dumped her out of town, in the middle of nowhere, it would give him more time.

Just as he was about to turn the key in the ignition, his phone rang.

"This is DC Brady, can I speak to Benjamin Peter Benson, please?"

A second interview was not good. It meant, at the very least, that he was under suspicion. They wanted him to come in right away. That wasn't good, either. No time to think things through. He'd kept calm, though. Casual as you please – he could read the cop's suspicions a mile off.

The appointment was for five o'clock. That gave him a couple of hours, at least. And if he didn't turn up, they'd wait a while. He started up the engine and, spinning the wheels, pulled out onto the road, heading away from town. The traffic would be heavy on the main road, but it was still the best route. If he was lucky, he might get as far as Maddington Woods.

The country lanes were deserted. He put his foot down and watched the needle on the accelerator gauge climb. Coming on to the roundabout too fast, the car skidded onto the slip road and Pete laughed. As he accelerated to join the carriageway, he heard Ellie say something. Was she coming round? He couldn't see. It didn't matter anyway – she'd be delirious for a good few hours yet. Plenty of time for him to get away. He shifted gear and the car lurched forward. Blood coursed through his veins and adrenaline kicked in. Pete Benson was King of the Road. What he needed was some music – something to drown out the moaning that was coming from the back seat. He switched on the radio and fiddled with the dial, taking his eyes off the road as he flicked through the stations.

The slip road was clear. In the wing mirror, there was a lorry approaching fast. If he put the pedal to the metal he could beat it, easily. Into fifth gear now and the engine caught, giving him what he needed. White lines flew past and the lane ahead narrowed. Checking the mirror again, there was something odd.

Something that didn't make sense. He'd passed the cab of the lorry. There it was behind him. So how come it was still there to his left?

A feeling of urgency focused his attention as he realised what he was seeing: There were two lorries. The radio played jazz. He hated jazz. Couldn't abide it. But there was no time to change it. Hunched forward over the steering wheel, he willed the car to make it. Cursed the lorry. Why didn't it move over? With his foot to the floor, he darted urgent glances between the wing mirror and the road ahead. Maybe he could do it. Moving past the second lorry, eating up the remaining metres too fast, knowing that the lorry would not now move over to give him space, he still believed there was time. Looking up, he saw the lorry driver's mouth working and heard the crushing blast of a horn, so close that it resonated through him. Get out of the fucking way! Just move, why can't you? The lorry driver was receding. It would be close. Fuck you, mate!

A saxophone filled Pete's head with a mellow, shifting tune as the world tipped over. He was falling at what must have been break-neck speed into a tunnel of long grass and bushes, but it seemed as though he were sliding for an eternity, aware that damage was being done to the side of the car, sensing metal twisting and buckling. All in slow motion. His hands still clutched the steering wheel. His legs hung useless in the footwell. His mind held on to the fading note as the radio burst out of its housing and died. *Fuck*! he thought, catching sight of his wasted, pale face in the rear view mirror. *Fuck, fuck, fuck.*

Chapter Twenty-two

When Benjamin Peter Benson didn't arrive at the police station, DC Brady waited for almost an hour before putting out a call for a patrol car to pick him up. It was police protocol to wait.

The flat where Benson lived seemed to be unoccupied.

"No one home, sir," said the reporting officer.

Will Brady was not surprised. "Alert all cars. He may be on the run. He mustn't get away."

"Understood."

There had been no word. It was late, and Will had gone home. There wasn't much else he could do.

It wasn't until early next morning that Will was informed that his chief suspect had gone missing from the scene of a road traffic accident. He'd been heading out of town when his vehicle had been struck by a lorry. That anyone had survived the wreck was, apparently, a miracle, according to the reporting officer.

The girl who had been travelling on the back seat was in a stable condition in intensive care, but the doctor Will spoke to, said that she wouldn't be able to answer any questions during the next twenty-four to forty-eight hours. The attending emergency services personnel had found no identification papers, which had prompted them to inform the police. Eventually.

"What next, Boss?" asked Will Brady. He didn't

like how things had gone so far. It was almost incredible to him that Ellie Braintree's identity had remained a mystery for almost twenty hours.

"Put as many resources as possible into the search for Benson. Maybe we're going to have to get Dominic Bryant back. See if he's around, will you?"

"You want to see him straight away?"

"Yes. If he can't come to us, we'll pay him a visit."

Alice Candy had already been worried that the situation might have shifted unexpectedly. She'd had a restless night, waking several times and thinking of Ellie – feeling that she was no longer in darkness, no longer confined in the same way, but not being able to tune in clearly to her thoughts. She'd phoned the station at midnight and again at three o'clock in the morning. Nothing had been reported. Connections had not been made. A car accident, a missing driver, a girl passed out on the back seat. It was hard to imagine how such a scenario could have failed to spark an urgent enquiry involving the police.

She'd thought more than once about contacting Will during the night, but decided that it would do no good. She'd imagined his voice, thick with sleep and then instantly alert. Pictured him dressing quickly and pulling up outside her house only to help push the case forward. Dedicated to his profession. Eager to be of assistance.

Now, Ellie was in hospital and Peter Benson had gone missing. That Ellie was alive, was a huge relief. That Benson had evaded detection was frustrating and ridiculous. That Will Brady, with his handsome profile and strong shoulders was concentrated one hundred per cent on finding the kidnapper and bringing him in, was just a little disappointing.

The inspector looked wistfully over to where Will was talking to one of the new investigators – a girl in her twenties with long blond hair. It was clear that the attraction was only one-way.

*****

Alice Candy had given little thought to her daughter's wedding, which would take place in four days' time. Instead, it had occupied her mind in a hidden corner, waiting to jump out and bite her at any moment. That she was guilty of neglect, was clear. That she had no choice in the matter, was her excuse and salvation.

The inspector sat at her desk, working out her latest idea of what had actually happened to Ellie Braintree, hoping that the girl would soon be able to tell her the whole story, when the telephone rang. Just for a moment, her intuition told her it would be Jude, phoning to say she'd missed something.

It was a call from Jayne Eade.

"Inspector Candy?"

"Speaking."

Mrs. Eade paused, then said, "I've got something you might be interested in."

Chapter Twenty-three

Dom left school as soon as he got the call – he'd returned to catch up on some administration – and went straight to the police station. It had been days since there'd been any news. Alice Candy had not returned his phone and had not managed to trace the call he'd made on it. He wished he had kept it. At least then he could have kept trying.

When he got to the station, there was an air of normality at reception that was at odds with the turmoil Dom felt was consuming him. The conversation seemed flippant. Even when Dom said who he was, the officer in charge was more interested in how many sugars her colleague was putting in her tea than informing Alice Candy that Dominic Bryant had dropped everything to come to the station urgently. Dom bit his tongue and checked his watch.

The policewoman noticed. "Just one moment, sir. If you'd like to take a seat, I'll inform the inspector that you are here."

Dom didn't move.

The officer hesitated, then picked up the phone. Less than a minute later, Will Brady arrived, walking quickly, and escorted him to the first floor, not slowing his pace before they reached Alice Candy's office.

"We have news that Ellie has been found."

Dom gaped, then smiled. His Ellie. Found.

"Where?" He looked from the inspector to the

constable and a sudden chill ran through him. "Is she all right?"

Alice Candy indicated a chair.

"She's in a bad way, I'm afraid, but stable."

Dom, who had been on the point of sitting down, stood up abruptly.

"Where is she? I want to see her."

"She's in hospital, Mr. Bryant. We've informed her parents. The doctors say she is out of danger, but that she's not allowed any visitors."

"I must see her."

Alice Candy had hoped he would stay long enough for her to put a proposition to him, but it was clear that he would not. "I understand. When you have seen her, Mr. Bryant, we would like to try something, and we need your help."

Dom nodded curtly, furious that he had wasted time coming to the police station instead of going straight to the hospital. He practically ran out of the office towards the stairs, taking them two at a time. Once inside his car, he drove too fast, his heart thumping, imagining Ellie lying helpless, wondering what terrible experiences she'd endured. He parked in a no-parking zone and sped into the hospital, past reception. He raced up the stairs and found Ellie's parents in an otherwise deserted corridor.

"We're not allowed to go in," said Ellie's mother, her eyes red and puffy, but still Ellie's eyes.

"Come with me, Dom," said Mr. Braintree, who had the appearance of a man in shock.

Ellie lay on her back, head raised, with an oxygen mask over her face and a drip attached to her arm. There was tape over her nose, which had been reset, and a large bruise bloomed on the side of her face. Her eyes were closed, and her chest barely rose when she breathed.

"Ellie," murmured Dom.

A nurse came out of the room and led them back along the corridor.

"She's resting. Try not to worry too much. We just need to flush the drugs out of her system and then she'll probably regain consciousness. Her injuries from the crash are superficial, mainly due to the fact that she was unconscious."

"What do you mean, *probably*?" asked Dom, wondering at the same time why Ellie should have drugs in her system.

"Almost certainly." The nurse put a hand on his arm.

"What drugs has she taken?" Dom wanted to know everything.

The nurse glanced up at Ellie's father, who spoke gently to Dom, "Come and have some sweet tea. It really helps. And I'll tell you all about it."

Dom went back to check on Ellie after he'd heard the full story. Of secondary concern was the whereabouts of her kidnapper. Dom guessed that Alice Candy wanted his help in apprehending the man who had left Ellie for dead at the side of the dual carriageway and so, after talking to Ellie's parents, he decided to see what he could do. Ellie would have wanted him to. He drove back to the police station contemplating what he would like to do to this man. Never had he been so angry.

This time, an officer took him up to the first floor straight away.

"Ah, thank you for coming back. I hope Ellie is comfortable?"

"Tell me how I can help."

Alice Candy hesitated. "Mr. Bryant, do you think that you will be able to remain in control of your emotions? We may only have one shot at contact. We don't know who has Ellie's phone, but we do know that last night, when we tried to make contact, as we have done on many occasions, without success, there was someone on the line. He didn't speak, but he did have the phone switched on. Not for long enough to get an accurate trace, unfortunately, although we do have a general location. The trace we managed to get proves that the house where Ellie was held is local."

"What have you got in mind, Inspector?"

"Well, that all depends..."

After Alice Candy had put forward her plan, Dom went back to the hospital. Ellie's dad had gone home to rest for a while and her mother was standing vigil.

"There's no change, I'm afraid, Dom."

Dom put an arm around her shoulders. She seemed less imposing than usual. As though just a little worn away. Dom supposed that having your daughter lying unconscious in intensive care could do that to you.

They made frequent trips along the corridor to stand outside the room where Ellie still lay unconscious, watching for signs. More than once, they thought they'd seen a twitch, a tiny movement, but the nurse had told them these were just nervous reactions, muscle spasms, and didn't signify a return to consciousness.

"The police want us to try Ellie's phone again," said Dom, when he and Ellie's mother had once more wandered back to the waiting area.

"Why do they want to do that, now that we've got her back?"

"They think that an accomplice of Benson's may have it. They've been trying on and off for a while now, and last night someone answered again. He didn't say anything, but the police think that if he were to hear my voice, he might recognise it and answer." Dom thought that maybe his voice would have the opposite effect. After all, when he'd spoken it had been to threaten, not cajole.

Ellie's mother looked at her hands and turned her wedding ring around on her finger.

"Do you think I should try?" asked Dom, finally.

"How about letting *me* try?" she said.

"*You*?"

"Yes. Why not? I sound just like Ellie. People are always getting us mixed up on the phone. Maybe whoever has her phone just wants to make sure she's all right. You know. Not..."

It was typical of Ellie's mum to see the good in people.

Dom didn't think for more than a moment. "That's not a bad plan. Brilliant, in fact. But do you think you'll be up to it?"

"I'm made of stronger stuff than you think, Dom."

Dom contacted Alice Candy, who gave the go ahead, saying that Ellie's mum would have to come in to the station so that, if the conversation could be kept going for long enough, the call could be more accurately traced. And so it was agreed that when Mr. Braintree returned, Dom and Mrs. Braintree would come to the station.

Not long after Dom had sat down again with a coffee from the machine, a doctor arrived to inform them that Ellie was awake.

Chapter Twenty-four

Joe was tired. He'd been watching over Donna for hours and she seemed no better. In fact, her breathing was so shallow that he almost thought she wasn't breathing at all. And if she didn't breathe, she would die. He took out the pot of paracetamol once more. Why weren't they helping? He'd read the instructions and given her three, every four hours. If he gave her another three, that would make nine altogether.

At least he still had Ellie's phone in his pocket. Donna's was on the charger in the kitchen, where Pete had plugged it in. Joe had tried to ring Pete, but he hadn't picked up. Even though Pete had left them, Joe was sure he would come back. He would come back more quickly if he knew Donna was getting worse. Joe had listened to the message on Pete's phone three times. "Ben Benson. I'm probably out on a job. Leave your number and I'll get back to you."

Ben Benson. That was his business name. But his friends called him Pete. Joe remembered what he'd said: *You can call me Pete, Joe.*

Joe was constantly aware of Ellie's phone. He felt the shape of it in his pocket, wanting to take it out. Sleek. Ellie had chosen it. She had good taste. When it had rung some hours earlier, he'd answered, thinking it might be Pete calling back. But it hadn't been, so after he'd listened to the man's voice for a moment, asking about Ellie, he'd switched it off again.

They can't trace it if it's switched off, Joe. Keep it switched off.

Very well, he would leave it switched off, but he was glad it was in his pocket, just in case he needed it.

There was a low groan from the bed. Joe sat down and looked into his sister's face. He eyelids fluttered as though she were trying to open them.

"Donna. Donna, can you hear me? It's Joe. Tell me what to do, Donna. I don't know what to do."

Donna always knew what to do. She'd kept him safe all his life. When people had called him names, she'd reassured him. *They're the morons. Not you, Joe.* If he'd had bad dreams, she'd sat with him until they went away, holding his hand and telling him stories. Stories about a boy called Joe, who was strong and brave. But now, he didn't feel strong or brave.

On a sudden impulse, he took out the phone, switched it on and tried Pete's number again. This time he left a message. *Donna's really sick. Please come back soon.* Just before he switched off, an icon flashed up on the screen. Joe knew what it meant: low battery power. He would not be able to call for much longer. It scared him to think that soon he and Donna would be all alone and unable to call anyone for help, locked away in the cellar.

"Donna. Wake up, *please*. Donna." He spoke quietly, watching her face for a response. But she had become very still again. At first, her eyes had flickered open from time to time and she'd even seen him, he was sure of it. What she'd said hadn't made sense, though. She sounded the same as she always did when she'd had too many glasses of wine, except then she fell over a lot and laughed all the time. Joe stroked her cheek with the back of his hand and took a deep breath that shook his body. She was sick. She could not help him. He was on his own.

Joe was hungry. He hadn't eaten for hours. When he was hungry, he couldn't concentrate. He needed to concentrate so that he could make decisions. The right decisions. Donna had taught him that life was about making the right decisions. She'd told him that sometimes, the right decisions were difficult to make. Sometimes you had to be strong to do the right thing and survive.

Joe needed to be strong. More than ever before in his whole life. And he needed to eat something so that he could think straight. *You can't think on an empty stomach, Joe.* That's what his mother had told him. *Feed the stomach to feed the mind.* If only his mother were here. If only she would open the door and put her arms around him. But she was far away and wouldn't be back for weeks. It was up to him to get his sister out of this mess.

Where could he get food? The tray that lay under the bed was empty, apart from two unopened drinks cartons. He drank one. He stood up and walked the length and breadth of the room, shining the lamp into every corner. There were some lines etched into the earth. He counted them and wondered what they meant. No food. And then he remembered that Donna had told him Ellie had made an emergency store. That she'd saved bread and biscuits and fruit in case the next tray didn't come. Donna had laughed at such a notion. Where had she said Ellie had put the food? Under the mattress. That was where she'd put it.

There wasn't much. An apple, three biscuits and a bread roll that was no longer fresh. As he ate, Joe thought about Ellie and hoped that Pete had wrapped her in a blanket so that she wouldn't be cold outside. He pictured her curled up in a field somewhere, not too far from the glittering lights of a village. Perhaps someone would find her. But he didn't think so. She might be hidden by long grass. And, what if she didn't wake up? What if she was sick, like Donna? Pete had given Ellie a lot of pills to make her forget. Maybe too many.

Joe took out the pot of medicine again. *They will make her feel better.* He shook three more pills into his hand. This time, there was a large round one sitting next to the small lozenge-shaped ones. Surely that couldn't be right? Inside the pot, there were six more small pills and no other big ones.

Joe remembered how Pete had stood with his back to him in the kitchen. He remembered the sound of the lid popping off, followed by the rattling of pills. Joe scowled. There was something not quite right about the view of Pete's back. Something not quite right about the movement of his shoulders, shaking in time with the rattling of the pills. Joe looked once more at the pills in his hand. The big one had some letters written across the middle. He raised the lamp and peered more closely at it, speaking the word aloud: *paracetamol*. What, then were the other pills? Joe thought he knew the answer to the question, but that would mean that Pete was not coming back. If Pete were not coming back they would both starve to death. So would Jessie.

Well then, he had no choice.

Chapter Twenty-five

Pete Benson didn't like being cornered. It would make things more difficult. All because of Donna and her crazy obsessions. Looking out from the bushes that surrounded the parking area at the front of his residential block, he clenched his fists and swore under his breath. His shoulder was painful and his knee swollen.

When the lorry had hit, the car had skidded off the edge of the slip road and ended up tilting dangerously into a drainage ditch more than fifty metres further along. It could have been worse. Pete had blinked several times, not knowing whether he'd been sitting suspended in his seat for an hour, a minute or a second. It soon became clear, though, that the accident had left him more or less uninjured and that he would have to get away before anyone turned up to help.

It had been exhausting getting back into town, going across fields, keeping low to avoid being spotted by the people who'd descended from the carriageway to find out what had happened. He was pretty sure that no one had seen him. When he got to a neighbouring village, he'd taken a bus into town. He hoped that no one would remember him. As it was market day, it wasn't likely.

Right now, he had other things on his mind. In the middle of the car park a police car, its lights flashing, blocked the front entrance. A couple of people stood next to their cars hoping to be allowed to leave. One of them, he knew: a bombastic authoritarian, who didn't approve of people like Pete – it would do him good to be kept waiting.

So, the police had his flat under surveillance and it was impossible to get in the front way. Everyone arriving or leaving through the communal entrance would be stopped. Pete cursed his luck. He was cold and he needed money, his passport and a change of clothes. He had to get inside somehow. Crouching low, he skirted the building and, staying hidden, observed the ancient twisting fire escape that led up the side of the flats. It was almost obscured by trees – if you didn't know where to look, you might not see it. The new steps were at the other end of the building, where a single police car stood and a policeman scanned the area leading onto the car park from the rear. There was no one close by and the flashing lights would make it difficult for the officer to notice movement in the distance, especially under cover of darkness and heavy foliage. It was worth the risk. There was no alternative, anyway.

He climbed up quickly, avoiding the broken steps and keeping to the centre to minimise the noise of creaking metalwork. He tapped on the unused fire door that led to the third floor. Down below, the solitary officer scanned the darkness with his flashlight in the other direction.

Pete tapped again and a woman wearing a pink dressing gown came out into the corridor, approached cautiously, and peered through the grimy safety glass. When she saw him, she smiled briefly and opened the door.

"Hey, Sal. Thanks."

"Hey, Pete. What've you done this time, eh? The

cops are swarming the place."

"You don't want to know."

"Need any help?"

"You could keep a lookout."

"Sure, no problem."

Pete's flat was two doors down. It was cordoned off with red and white tape.

"The place was busy earlier, but I don't think there's anyone in there now. Shall I go see?" Sal spoke in low tones. She strolled casually down the corridor, looking this way and that. She tried Pete's door and shook her head. It was locked. The coast was clear.

Making short work of the newly installed padlock, Pete entered the flat, filling a rucksack with clothes while Sal kept watch. He took a wad of cash from the bookshelf and another from a shoe in his wardrobe. He slipped his passport into a zipped pocket. The police were idiots.

When he came out, clicking the lock shut again, Sal put a hand on his arm and looked into his face with a grin. "You've got my number," she said.

"Sure have, Sal. You're a life saver, you know that?"

She smiled again and held open the door to the fire escape. As Pete passed in front of her, he slid an arm around her and kissed her on the lips.

"Call me," she whispered into the night.

The sky was clear and the temperature would soon drop. It wasn't far to Jerry's house along the back streets. It wasn't a night to be out for long, even though it was still summer. A fine drizzle came down and blew in gusts on a chill wind. If he'd dumped Ellie, she might not have made it, lying all night on the sodden ground. As it was, she had a chance. When he'd left her, she'd been alive, her body wedged behind the front seats. She'd probably be fine. As for Donna, if her idiot brother kept feeding her the pills, she would be out for a couple of days. When Pete got far enough away and sorted out a plan, he'd make a call to the police. There was water in the cellar. People could survive without food for weeks, as long as they kept hydrated.

He felt no guilt. The shit she'd put him through, she deserved it. But Joe? Now that would be a pathetic sight. The boy would be a blubbering wreck. If he could put two and two together, he might come up with something. But Joe wouldn't put two and two together. No way.

The main thing was that Pete would be in the clear. With Donna and Joe out of the picture for a while, and Ellie, even if she recovered, not knowing where she'd been or Donna's true identity, he was laughing. So, why was he running? Easy. There was no way he was turning himself in. Not when he could get away. He'd had enough experience of the police to know that they would use any trick in the book to put him back in prison. Once was enough in anyone's lifetime.

When Pete got to Jerry's he showered and changed while Jerry sent out for a takeaway.

"I need a lift to the station," said Pete, as he cleaned up his plate with a piece of bread.

"No problem. When d'you want to go?"

"Round about now."

"Sounds bad."

"Nothing I can't handle."

It was most unlikely that the police would be checking the trains, but Jerry gave Pete a pair of sunglasses and a white stick. He used it to claim disability benefit.

"How d'you get away with it?" Pete laughed.

"Impaired vision, mate."

"How bad is it?"

"What do *you* think? As long as The Social is none   the   wiser,   it   suits   me."

Sitting on the train with the stick resting between his legs, Pete couldn't help grinning every time someone stared. A young girl helped him onto the platform at Porthmadog and a middle-aged couple offered him a lift into town, which he accepted.

It was amazing how much people were willing to help a blind man. And how chatty they all were! Curious, he supposed. They'd remember him for sure. And that was what he wanted. If they remembered the blind man, then any search for Peter Benson would come to nothing.

In the phone store, he almost got caught out. Almost. But the assistant had smiled when he'd said he had impaired vision, that he wasn't totally blind. He would be able to make out the numbers on the keypad if they were large enough.

With his old phone crushed and residing in an industrial dustbin at the back of Jerry's building, Pete was untraceable. No one knew where he'd gone and no one knew who he was. Pete. That was his name. No more odd jobbing for a while. Ben Benson would disappear and nobody would give a damn. He'd rent a caravan and lie low. Grow a beard, wear his hair long. Keep the stick and the glasses. Then he'd move on. Get some new business cards printed. Blend in to a new community. Simple. Maybe he'd hop over to Ireland. There'd be no chance of anyone there co-operating with the police. Not when he told them his grandfather had been an Irish farmer with seven mouths to feed.

So, having eaten a good lunch in a local cafe, he strode out along the coastal road occasionally tapping his stick in front of him when cars passed by, and soon came to a camping sign. There were two caravans for rent. It was the end of the summer season and the proprietor was happy to let out a two berth for a month at a fraction of the high season tariff. Especially to a man who clearly had problems of his own.

"If you need anything..."

"I'll be fine. Thank you."

The local man watched his new tenant negotiate the single step and unlock the caravan door without any trouble. Inside, Pete threw down his stick, removed his glasses and made tea with the supplies he'd brought from the town. Soon the kettle whistled and he was sitting behind net curtains looking out over the Irish Sea.

Chapter Twenty-six

Alice Candy was closing in. What she needed was direct contact with someone who could visualise Peter Benson. Sometimes, if she could get a good reaction, there was a connection. She couldn't explain it. It just happened.

Ellie was disoriented and had sustained substantial bruising. In spite of this, she looked stable enough.

The inspector listened patiently to the doctor's diagnosis – he was satisfied that the rohypnol Ellie had been given had been almost entirely flushed from her system, but wanted to keep her in for another twenty four hours to make sure there were no further complications. She would have to be monitored at home, too. It was possible to experience a seizure weeks later, after taking such a drug.

After giving Alice Candy a knowing look, he reluctantly granted her twenty minutes to interview Ellie. The hunt for Benjamin Peter Benson was on. Pete Benson, Ben Benson – whatever he wanted to call himself – would be brought in, and soon, if she had anything to do with it.

The room was quiet and bright. There was sunlight on the polished floor and a profusion of dust motes floating in the air. Ellie's eyes were closed.

"Hello, Ellie. My name is Inspector Candy and this is DC Brady. Do you feel strong enough to answer some questions?"

Ellie opened her eyes and smiled as though the words had come gently to her from far away. She spoke clearly, but with unnatural care. It must be the sedation.

"I'm not thinking too well, but I'm sure I can tell you a few useful things."

Alice Candy pulled up a chair and Will stood on the other side of the bed with his notebook at the ready.

"What I need to know is information about the person or people who abducted you. We think we know who one of them is, but a description, or anything he or the other person said might help us to find them. I'll be recording the conversation, if that's all right, and my colleague will be taking notes."

Will nodded, smiling.

Ellie nodded her consent and began to speak. "I don't remember being taken. Not a thing. The first memory I have is of sitting on a bench outside the allotments. Then, I woke up in a cellar. In between, I've tried, but there's nothing."

Alice Candy placed her hand on Ellie's arm. "A cellar? Can you describe it?"

"Yes. I got to know every corner of that bunker. And I can tell you about the girl I shared it with, too."

Will looked up for a moment and Alice Candy saw flecks of gold in his hair.

"That would be helpful," she said, allowing her eyes to close a little and preparing to enter the cellar with Ellie, already flaring her nostrils at the now familiar earthy smell.

"Go ahead, Ellie. We're listening," said Will Brady.

Ellie recalled everything, wondering a little at the way Alice Candy occasionally tightened the grip on her arm.

"She's tuning in," explained Will, smiling reassuringly. "Just go with it."

Ellie focused on the young officer, who asked questions and noted down her responses. She told him that Donna's real name was Amanda Leighton and that she had known her years ago at school; that her brother Joe had delivered trays of food to the cellar and brought fresh clothing. She told him about the drugs in Donna's pocket and how she had tried to use them to make an escape. And she didn't forget the violence she'd suffered at Peter Benson's hands.

Inspector Candy opened her eyes and said, "So, it was Donna, Amanda Leighton, who engineered all this? It sounds as though she had problems of her own."

Ellie described Mandy's odd, obsessive behaviour at junior school and how she had been generally disliked.

"I don't know whether Mandy, Amanda, did it on her own. I think the man, Pete, was heavily involved too. He was the one I felt most threatened by. He was the one who made me swallow the pills. As for Joe, he didn't really understand, I don't think. He was kind. He had difficulties... he was childlike."

Alice Candy agreed. "Yes. Your description of his part in this would seem to suggest that he was not fully aware of what his sister and Benson were doing."

Ellie looked the inspector in the eye. "Will you find them?"

"It's been difficult. But now that you've given us a name, I'm hoping we'll be able to progress more easily. We have a plan too, Ellie. May I tell you about it?"

When Alice Candy had left, Dom came back into the room and sat beside Ellie, taking her hand.

"Do you know what's happening next?"

"Yes, Inspector Candy told me. Dom, *I* could do it. I don't want Mum to be upset any more."

"You'd have to come to the station. That's where the equipment for tracing the call is."

Ellie was about to say that she would be strong enough to come, that she insisted on doing it herself, when the phone in Dom's pocket rang.

Chapter Twenty-seven

It was raining. The kind of rain that came down in rods, drumming on the roof of the caravan, lashing against the window. Welsh weather. Pete had been cooped up all day. More and more, he believed it was time to move on. He'd been in the caravan for just three days and already he was climbing the walls. And it was tedious to have to always remember to wear dark glasses and carry his white stick.

And to add to his discomfort, Mr. Davis was outside, calling him. Hammering on the door. Pete put on his glasses and opened up. There he was, with a cagoule zipped up to his chin. Behind him was a police car.

The look on Mr. Davis' face was almost comical. Pete went back inside, gathered his things and stepped down into the mud, dropping the keys into his landlord's hand.

"Thanks, Mr. Davis."

Two constables got out of the car to join the officer who stood next to Mr. Davis. One of them stepped forward, instructed Benson to turn around and snapped on a pair of handcuffs, while another read him his rights. The rain had soaked through Benson's clothing by this time – he knew that there would be no hurry to get him out of the rain. The policemen were equipped with waterproofs, after all. Eventually, one of them opened the rear door and pushed Benson's head down as he slid into the back seat. Pete's amused expression had not drawn them, as the officer in charge had pronounced the words he was required to repeat.

Mr. Davis had retreated to his site office, and still stared out at the scene from his window.

Inside the car, the windows needed clearing and the sound of the fan was loud at first. Little was said on the journey back. Benson's request to have his handcuffs removed was denied. The officer in the front passenger seat radioed that Benson had been apprehended without incident, and a response came that someone by the slightly ridiculous name of Candy, would be waiting to meet him at the station.

Pete hardly gave a thought to Donna or Joe. There was no way the police would find them, even if Ellie had spilled the beans. He doubted whether anyone would miss them, either. No jobs. No neighbours. No friends. He would find a way to let the police know their whereabouts in good time. All in good time. Ellie would not be able to say anything much. Nothing incriminating, anyway. Her word against his. They wouldn't be able to hold him more than forty-eight hours. If push came to shove, he'd get Jerry on board, but for the moment, the police had nothing. And he was used to their bully boy tactics. He wouldn't crack. He could wait it out.

When the car pulled up and he got out, there was a tall, slim attractive woman with a serious look on her face. She was dolled up in a pink dress and matching high heels. Not bad. Not bad at all. She spoke to one of the constables and then looked directly at Pete. Inspector Candy – must be. She signed a piece of paper held out to her on a clipboard and gave it back, putting a hand on the shoulder of the officer who

157

accompanied her.

Alice Candy, recently returned from her daughter's wedding, called away just after the toasts had been made, but before the feasting had commenced, turned and went back inside the station.

"That the boss?" grunted Pete.

"Inspector Candy to you, Benson."

"Bit of a looker, then?"

The officer ignored him.

There was an aroma of freshly brewed coffee as Pete entered the station. The officer who stood to his left wasn't the type to offer him a cup.

"Ready for him straight away? Or shall we put him in a cell for a while?" he asked his colleague at reception.

Tactics. Make him sweat. They didn't scare Pete.

"They want him upstairs, pronto."

"Okay. Mine's black with two sugars. Any biscuits?"

"New box. Luxury assortment." The officer behind the desk glanced at Benson with the smuggest of grins.

*****

After the formalities had been observed, Alice Candy began the interview. She had never been fond of following accepted protocol: keeping the suspect in the dark, hoping he or she would slip up, eliciting information with routine questions that wore a person down. The tried and trusted methods succeeded some of the time, but the inspector favoured a more intuitive approach – she was more like a safe breaker, alive to minute changes in pressure and resistance, she would turn the dial one step further than anticipated, then pull on the handle to expose what lay within. This time, she blew off the sides with a bombshell.

"Mr. Benson, what can you tell us about Amanda Leighton?"

It was clear that Peter Benson had been ready for most things, but not for this.

Alice Candy did not miss a beat. "I notice from your expression that you are familiar with the name, Mr. Benson?"

Benson hesitated then said, "No comment."

"I see. That's the way you want to play it. Then I shall tell you some of what we already know. It might save a bit of time."

Benson sat up in his chair, crossed his legs and placed one hand on top of the other.

The inspector saw through this show of nonchalance and continued seamlessly with her exposé of the facts. "Amanda Leighton, otherwise known as Donna Barnes, is a young woman who has a personality disorder. A mild form of schizophrenia. At the age of five, she was fostered by Mrs. Sandra Barnes, who also has a son called Joe – a young man who has moderate learning difficulties."

"No comment."

"I wasn't aware that I had asked for one, Mr. Benson. Should you wish to correct me, or add something I have neglected to mention, I should be obliged if you would wait for an appropriate interval."

Benson rolled his shoulders back, cricked his neck to one side and raised his eyes to the clock above Alice Candy's head. He had begun to sweat.

Alice Candy took a sip of the iced water that stood on her desk, before continuing. "As I was saying,

Amanda joined her new family at the age of five and it wasn't until the age of sixteen that she opted to officially change her name to Barnes. She changed her Christian name at the same time, as you may or may not be aware."

Benson looked out into the open plan office beyond the glazed partition walls that separated him for the bustle of normal life, and let out a yawn.

"Are we keeping you awake, Mr. Benson? Perhaps you would like DC Brady to bring you a cup of coffee? I believe you have a preference for Lavazza. Black. Two sugars."

This time her suspect could not contain his surprise and his mouth fell open a little as, simultaneously, Will Brady handed him a handkerchief, gesturing that he should wipe the perspiration from his brow.

Alice Candy went on as though Benson and Donna were her specialist subjects.

"I believe that you first met up with Donna at a local cinema. She was twenty at the time. It was an evening showing, and there was a clear sky with a full moon. What was the name of the film, Detective Constable Brady?"

Will Brady referred to his notebook. "The Woman in Black."

"Ah, yes. Did you enjoy the film, Mr. Benson?"

"No comment."

"Of course." Alice Candy let out a small sigh. She closed her eyes and her nostrils flared. "Funny how such a film inspires fear: the smell of damp earth, the terrible sensation of being trapped underground." She opened her eyes and looked directly at Benson, who seemed to be waiting for her to go on.

The inspector raised her eyebrow and Will nodded

almost imperceptibly. He finished the notes he was taking and turned to Benson with a wide grin.

"She's quite something, isn't she?"

Benson sparked into life once more, sitting straighter in his chair, speaking fast. "You've got nothing. I had no part in any of it. Either charge me, or let me go. I know my rights."

Alice Candy took up the questioning again, giving Will a severe look as she began. "Just as soon as we sort out some details, Mr. Benson. Now, let's get down to the real business in hand, shall we? We know about Ellie, of course. We know you gave her enough rohypnol to endanger her life. We know you abandoned your car after an accident on the road out of town, and that you ran away, deserting Ellie without the slightest concern for her welfare. There are witnesses, Mr. Benson, who have given sworn statements."

"I don't know what you're talking about. My car is in an allocated parking space outside my flat."

"Is this yours, Mr. Benson?" Will held up a grey hooded jacket. The one Pete had been wearing when he'd had the accident. The one he'd asked Jerry to dispose of.

"Never seen it before." New beads of perspiration formed on his brow.

"Your friend Jerry left it in the bins at the back of his apartment block. Rather careless, wouldn't you say?" Asked the inspector, pleasantly.

"Is that all you've got? An old grey jacket that I might have worn once?"

Will sat on the corner of the desk and leaned in, putting his face nearer Benson's. "The car left at the scene of the accident was registered in Donna's name. But I assume you drove it from time to time, as your

161

fingerprints have been found all over the interior?"

Pete didn't look at the constable, but stared blankly at the inspector. He spoke with new reassurance. "I sometimes took it out, yeah. Don't know anything about a crash, though."

Inspector Candy flipped distractedly through some papers on her desk and asked, "So, your relationship with Donna, Mr. Benson. Is it ongoing?"

"No comment."

"Let's talk about the drugs you gave Ellie, then. Where did you get them?"

"No comment."

"Ellie tells us that Donna had a supply in her pocket, when they were locked up together. Is that correct, to your knowledge?"

Benson didn't stumble over his words. "She took drugs, yeah. I don't know which ones."

"I believe that you have already served a two year sentence for supplying drugs for sale to the public, Mr. Benson?"

"No comment."

"I see. And what about Joe? Did he take drugs?"

"Not to my knowledge, no."

"Do you happen to have your phone with you, Mr. Benson?"

"Yes."

"May I see it? Ellie still hasn't found hers."

Peter Benson grinned and reached into his pocket. "Sure. Take it."

Alice Candy gave it a cursory glance and passed it to DC Brady, who went out of the room. For a long moment, there was silence. Then, out of the blue:

"Do you know the whereabouts of Joe and Donna Barnes, Mr. Benson?"

"No."

"Are they perhaps locked away in the cellar at their own home?"

"No comment."

"The home that has a green front door, with a red tiled entrance leading up three steps to a farmhouse kitchen?"

Once more, Benson couldn't hide his emotions, it was obvious that had counted on having more time to get away. "No comment!"

DC Brady returned with the phone and placed it on the desk in front of Peter Benson, whose eyes were now wide with something akin to terror.

"Ah, yes, Mr. Benson, I'm sure you're wondering how we know so much. Perhaps you believe we are leading you into a trap? I can assure you, there is no need for such subterfuge. We have found them, Mr. Benson, that is the long and short of it."

The phone rang, once, twice, three times.

"Why don't you answer it? It can only be for you."

He picked up the phone and pushed the appropriate button.

"Is that you Pete? It's Joe, here. Donna says you made a mistake with the paracetamol."

Alice Candy chose this moment to place an empty can of Sprite, sealed in a specimen bag, in the centre of her desk. Next to it, she placed a smaller bag with a ring pull inside it. Both had been dusted for fingerprints. Jayne Eade had cleaned the van, but Andrew had forgotten to put the rubbish out for collection.

"Thirsty, Mr. Benson?" asked Will Brady.

Chapter Twenty-eight

Dom knocked on Ellie's door at seven thirty. The lights were on at the front of the house. That was good. When she opened the door, he kissed her and handed her the present he'd bought for her birthday weeks earlier. The bruises on her face had almost disappeared, but Dom knew that it would take time for the Ellie he had known, the girl who was confident and spontaneous, without a care in the world, to come back fully.

"Thanks." Ellie held the gift, unsure what to do with it. Then, she laughed.

Dom laughed too. "Shall we go? You can open it in the car."

Ellie locked up the house, double checking, and then she turned and took Dom's hand. Her small hand in his. The way it had been and would always be.

"Nando's?"

"Lovely. I'm starving."

In the car, Ellie opened her present distractedly. Dom supposed it was less exciting to receive surprises so long after your birthday. But, when she saw the necklace, she let out a small gasp.

"Hope you like it."

"It's lovely."

Dom looked across. "Did you speak to Inspector Candy today?"

Ellie answered without hesitation. "Yes. I'm not

going to prosecute Donna."

Dom nodded the way people do when they get the response they'd expected. He had known she would not. That didn't mean he had to like it, though.

"Are you sure about this, Ellie?"

"Yes. I've spoken to Donna's psychiatrist and she says that if she had to go through a trial, with the chance of being put in prison, it would probably end badly for her and for Joe. This way, she'll get help. She'll be under supervision and she'll be able to see Joe regularly. He's been given a studio flat near where Donna will be treated. Dr. Wilkinson says that she should make a full recovery, now that Benson isn't around. He's the monster. Not Donna."

This was too much. "How can you be so sure about her?"

"You don't understand, Dom. She's had a very difficult life…"

There was nothing he could say to make her change her mind.

"…and Joe needs his sister. I'm not going to be the one to take her away from him."

Dom felt a tightness in his chest. Why did Ellie always have to put other people's well-being before her own?

Something drove him on. He tried to keep the irritation from his voice. "Doesn't Joe have anyone else? Donna doesn't seem like a very good role model."

"Don't think so."

"And what about Benson?" he asked, pulling up at traffic lights and studying Ellie's profile for a long moment.

She didn't look at him, but stared out at the road ahead. "They say he'll be charged with kidnapping and maybe even attempted murder. Probably get around five years."

The lights changed and he moved off. "Doesn't seem much."

Ellie put a hand on his knee as they arrived and parked outside the restaurant. This time, she fixed him with her beautiful, troubled eyes. "I'm just glad it's all over… Can we talk about something else tonight?"

He was sorry he'd brought the whole thing up on Ellie's belated birthday treat. How thoughtless he'd been!

"Sure. Sorry." He smiled and changed the subject. "Have you thought about what you'll do when your parents go back to Spain?"

"I was hoping to talk to you about that over dinner. How do you fancy sharing?"

Before they got out of the car, Dom pulled Ellie towards him and kissed her. Nothing would come between them again. Nothing, and no one.

Chapter Twenty-nine

"Hi, Joe. Wow!"

"Hello, Donna." Joe let himself be hugged.

"Jess!" She crouched down and petted an excited Jess. "How d'you like your new home, then? Where's your basket, eh?"

Joe stood by, feeling a little overwhelmed. "Jessie sleeps upstairs in my room. She doesn't like to be left alone, do you Jess?"

Donna straightened up and glanced around the room. "Very cosy. Very tasteful. How do I look?"

The question took him rather by surprise. Of course, he had noticed that she looked different as soon as she'd come in. She had changed her hairstyle and dyed her hair auburn. She was wearing a new black coat and a belt with a silver buckle at the front. She looked nice.

"Smart. Very smart." Joe pulled his jumper straight and ran his fingers through his hair.

Donna gave him a quick smile. "You've got a great place here, you know?" She wandered around, picking up things he had placed on shelves, smirking a little. She handled a wire model of a bicycle he'd made, then put it back the wrong way round. "Yeah. You've made it nice. Very nice."

He adjusted the ornament. Couldn't help himself. Saw the look on his sister's face.

A bright new thought struck him, and he said, "It's got a spare bedroom, for when you can ..." Joe didn't really know how to finish the sentence. "When can you stop living at the centre, Donna?"

"Not long now, Joe. Listen, can you do me a favour?"

"What do you want me to do?" He had known there would be something.

"There's a girl I know. Charlie. She's got something for me. I want you to take this to her and bring back the packet she'll give you."

He considered the envelope. "What is it, Donna?"

"It's a secret, Joe." She put a finger to her lips. "No one must know about it. Top secret."

"Why can't *you* go and get it?"

Donna flung herself into an armchair and sighed. As she undid the buttons on her coat, she shook her head slowly. "Bloody hell, Joe. I thought we were best friends."

"We are! You are my sister *and* my best friend, but…"

"*But what*? We help each other, don't we? If we can't rely on each other, who *can* we rely on, eh? What do we always say?"

He trotted out the words she was waiting to hear: "You save me, I save you."

That's right. Exactly right. We can't trust other people. You know that."

Joe frowned. "Not even Dr. Wilkinson?"

"No. Especially not Dr. Wilkinson."

"But she's helping you. She's making you better."

"Listen, Joe. There's nothing wrong with me. I didn't do anything bad, did I? It was all Pete. Yeah? All I wanted was to spend some time with Ellie. She said she was my friend, and she lied."

He didn't understand. "Ellie is a nice person, Donna. She helped us. Inspector Candy said…"

"I know what she said, Joe. I know what she said. Don't you understand? They want to control us. So they tell us stories to keep us quiet. Ellie lied to me. Just like Pete. And Inspector Candy and Dr. Wilkinson are lying too. They don't care about us. They won't let us be together. Not soon, maybe not ever."

His legs felt weak and his head was spinning with all this new information. He sat down and Jess jumped up onto his lap.

Donna leaned forward, and her voice sounded as though she were telling Joe another secret. He didn't want to be told another secret.

"Don't worry. We'll be okay. I just have to play along. I know what Dr. Wilkinson wants to hear. If I can get the medicine I need, I can make it. I just need you to help me get the medicine, Joe."

He gazed at his sister and stroked Jess, saying, "It's okay, Jessie. We'll be okay."

All the calmness had gone out of his head, and he was feeling confused. Before Donna had arrived, his life had felt easy, perhaps for the first time. The dinner was almost ready, there was a bottle of white wine in the fridge and he'd bought ice cream for dessert. He looked over at the table, set with new place mats and shiny cutlery, two glasses, polished with a clean tea towel the way his mother had taught him.

Suddenly, all of it seemed meaningless. His sister was telling him things that messed everything up again.

"What are we going to do, Donna? I thought Dr. Wilkinson was going to make you better so that you could come and live with Jessie and me."

"We have to be clever, Joe. I can do what they

169

want. I can jump through their hoops. Then, when they say I'm better, we can go somewhere. Together. But first, I want Ellie to know that she won't get away with what she's done. She has to be punished, Joe. Pete's in prison because of her. I'm not allowed to live here with you because of her. We can't go home because of her."

"But Pete is a bad man. He locked the door and left us. You were sick. He made me give you pills that made you sicker."

"I know he was bad, Joe. But he was coming back. It was Ellie who left us. She's going to pay for what she did to me. To us."

"Ellie was sick too. Pete gave her..."

Donna jumped out of the chair and stood over him. "Just *shut up*, Joe. You don't know what you're talking about. You mustn't listen to anyone but *me*. When the police came to find us, you should have held your tongue. You told them too much. What did I say to you? *Not a word! Don't say anything!*" She paused, before continuing in a gentler voice. "But I forgive you, Joe. I know you didn't mean to get me and Pete into trouble. I know that."

They ate dinner in sombre mood. Joe didn't want to upset Donna, but he knew that something was very wrong. Donna wasn't seeing things straight. But she was his sister. What could he do about it? When he tried to tell her she was wrong, she got angry. Who could he turn to for help, if there was no one he could trust?

He served the ice cream without any pleasure. The meal was spoiled. Donna didn't give him chance to say anything, but just spoke faster and faster, even when she had food in her mouth. She said they would pack a suitcase and go abroad. It would be exciting. They would take out the money their mother had left them in the special bank account. They would both need to sign to get the money. Later they would get money for the house and live on the proceeds. For the moment they had enough to last a long, long time.

Joe wanted to ask her when their mother was coming back. How could they get money for the house when it didn't belong to them? He tried to tell Donna that they should stay where they were and wait for her. She would be worried if they went abroad without her.

"No, Joe. She left us too. Understand? She went away and she's not coming back."

This, Joe knew to be false. Donna was not herself. She should finish her treatment. Then they could go back to the house if they wanted to, or stay in the flat. Their mother would come home and be nearby. Donna could get a job as a secretary, and he would look for work, too. Bella, his counsellor, had said there were jobs that he could do, once he got settled. Part-time work. She had smiled and said that he was a 'people person'. The thought of a job excited him. But, when he mentioned this to Donna, she said that Bella was just trying to trick him.

At the end of the visit, she put her arms around his neck and kissed his cheek. Her eyes bore into him when she spoke. "I need you to get the package. All right, Joe? Charlie'll be sitting on a bench along the far side of the river, where the main entrance to the park is. She'll be wearing a yellow jacket. Okay? Give her the envelope and put the package in your pocket. Tomorrow, at two pm. Then come straight back here. I'll let myself in. Remember, I have to be back at the centre by four. I'm counting on you, Joe.

Don't let me down, will you?"

When Donna had gone, Joe cleared the kitchen and made hot chocolate. The flat was peaceful again and he was able to think. He went over the things that Donna had said, talking to Jess, who looked just as confused as he was.

"Don't worry, Jessie. I'll look after you. Just don't say anything, okay?" He laughed at the way Jess was looking at him.

Later, as he sat in front of the television, Joe remembered the happiness and relief he'd felt when the door to the cellar had been forced by the police, and Donna had been taken away in an ambulance. At the hospital, the doctors said that she wouldn't have lasted much longer; that the drugs Pete had given to Joe had not been paracetamol, but rohypnol and that Donna's body had been poisoned. They would have to remove the poison from her blood with liquids that dripped down a tube into her arm. She would be all right, though. She would be all right thanks to the call that Joe had made on Ellie's phone. He remembered reading the flashing sign on the screen. The phone would have died if he'd waited. And so might he and Donna.

It was a terrible thing to have to do: to go against what Donna had told him. But, he'd done it anyway. To save her. Why couldn't she see things the way he did?

He took the envelope from the table, opened it and counted out the money. Thirty pounds. Joe wondered how many pills you could buy with thirty pounds. He wondered what kind of pills they would be and why Donna wanted to take them.

That night, he lay awake for hours. He couldn't

stop thinking about what Donna had said about Ellie. That she had lied. That Ellie had said she was Donna's friend, when she wasn't really. And for the first time, he saw clearly that Ellie had been a prisoner. That the cellar had been a frightening place for her. That no matter how comfortable he'd tried to make her, no matter how nice the trays he'd prepared had been, she'd wanted to get out. To get out and get away from Donna. It was Donna who was bad. His sister. But she was bad because she was sick. That's what Bella said. She was sick, and with Dr. Wilkinson's help, she would get better.

No matter what happened, the most important thing was that Donna should get better. And with this thought, Joe was able to sleep.

Chapter Thirty

Ellie was glad to be out. Life had almost returned to normal. Almost. She'd talked it over with Dom and he'd said that they should try living under the same roof for a while. That had been more than a month ago. It had made her stomach turn over with joy, and just a hint of terror. Not the terror she'd felt in the cellar, when she'd wondered if she would ever see him again. Maybe terror was the wrong word entirely. In fact it was difficult to pinpoint the emotion she had when she walked around the house and imagined how different it would seem with Dom there too.

Anyway, tonight was the night he was moving in. After work, he'd said. And she wanted to cook a nice dinner to welcome him properly. There was that feeling again, in her stomach!

Her parents had been all for it when she'd telephoned them. She had heard music in the background, and after a rather perfunctory chat with her father, he had called her mother to the phone. She'd been swimming in the communal pool. Ellie imagined her smiling. *What a good idea, darling!* The details were discussed. There was plenty of extra space if they wanted to pop over from Spain. Her father had not actually said so, but Ellie knew that he didn't like the idea of her being alone in the house after her ordeal. *Just let us know if you need anything, you know, for the house… or for you.*

It would be fine. Exciting.

Outside, Ellie could breathe more freely. These days, she couldn't get enough fresh air into her lungs and today, as sometimes happened, she felt almost intoxicated by it. It made her want to laugh out loud. Above her, there was the sky, and beyond that, the universe went on forever. She'd never really thought about it before. Being locked up certainly made you think about that kind of thing. Ellie knew that the universe had no beginning and no end. That was the way it had to be. No limits. No doors with locks. She took another deep breath and almost flung her arms out to the sides with happiness.

The walk into town was invigorating and when she got there the market was crowded with shoppers. Mothers with their small children, teenagers in groups, older couples out together, smartly dressed and quietly browsing the stalls. There were people she knew, who wanted to ask how she was. People who had read about her in the newspapers, who didn't stop, but smiled and nodded from a distance. So many people had asked her the same question that now she just answered that she was much better, thank you. All right now, yes. Thank you for asking. Dom's mother had told her not to say too much; not to get involved in long conversations. It had been very good advice.

It had been just about six weeks since she'd come home and the time she'd spent in the cellar had become less and less real to her. She still remembered it, of course, but it was as though it had happened to someone else. Her counsellor had said it was part of a perfectly normal healing path. Ellie didn't know about healing paths, but she liked to listen to Rebecca's voice, which washed over her, making her feel strong and sure. And safe.

A woman bumped into Ellie and turned to smile and apologise. Yes. This was the real world, and these people were ordinary people, out at the market, as she was, to do a little shopping. And the future was real too, now that she and Dom were going to be living together – the thought of it made her tingle all over. No terror, this time. Just joy.

Ellie looked around the stalls and bought the things she needed for the meal that night: mushrooms as big as dinner plates and crumbly blue cheese cut fresh and wrapped in greaseproof paper. Garlic, large and pungent, and crisp, freshly dug-up lettuce for the salad. The other things she needed were already in the cupboard at home, along with a bottle of Cava chilling in the fridge.

There was a stall she'd passed a couple of times and now she went back to it to look at a purse she knew she couldn't resist, made of pale pink leather with a tiny owl for a clasp. Rebecca had said she should be nice to herself and so she bought that, too. It thrilled her to look at it and know it was hers to keep. It would belong to her new life.

As Ellie looked up, she saw a girl on the other side of the square, who, just for a moment, reminded her of Donna. The sensation was instant and shocking. It made her stomach turn over. The girl's hair was a different colour, but the way she moved and the set of her head and shoulders sent a shockwave through Ellie. Donna, here at the market. It wasn't a pleasant thought. She watched as the girl walked away and took the hand of a small child, Ellie relaxed. Not

Donna. Rebecca had warned her about the kind of paranoia that could make her see things that were not really there. This too would be temporary.

It's not Donna. It's just a woman with her child.

Donna is not a bad person.

Ellie calmed herself and wandered round the stalls a little longer, thinking more rationally about what had become of the girl she'd spent so much time with in the cellar room, glad that she was getting professional help, glad that she would one day be able to lead a normal life, away from people like Peter Benson.

A couple passed by with a small dog on a lead. The red coat it was wearing reminded Ellie of Jess. Joe and Jess were living not far away, she'd heard. It would be good for Joe to have his own life, at last. But Ellie worried that he would miss his sister. She worried that he would perhaps blame Ellie for what had happened. That was not important really, though. It was a selfish thought. One day, she mused, Joe and Donna would be reunited and they would be able to live their lives in peace, away from people like Benson. He was bad through and through. Peter Benson had left Donna and Joe to die, of this she was certain.

"Hello, Ellie."

Ellie jumped. "Oh, hello Mr. Roberts."

"Doing some shopping, I see! Good to be out, isn't it?"

Out of the cellar. "Yes. Very good."

"How are you feeling, Ellie?" Mr. Robert's face

had sunk just a little.

What to say? I feel as though I'm here in the real world, but also stuck in the story of a girl who was locked up in a dark cellar. "Much better, thank you!"

"Good. That's good. Say hello to your parents for me, will you? I'll bet they're sitting round the pool, sipping cocktails!"

There was something macabre about Mr. Robert's smile. *Could a person like Mr. Roberts keep a girl under lock and key?*

Ellie realised too late that she hadn't spoken. The man who was waiting for her reply was suddenly a stranger to her.

"Are you all right, Ellie?"

"What? Oh, yes. Yes, thank you. I thought I saw someone, that's all."

The man smiled hesitantly. It was obvious that he felt awkward and wanted to get away. That he regretted speaking to her. His smile was brave, but frozen. "Okay, then. Nice to see you, dear. Enjoy your day, Ellie. Got to get going." He raised a hand and made to place it on her shoulder.

Don't touch me! She recoiled just a little, before coming to her senses. "Yes, thank you, Mr. Roberts. I'm sorry…"

"That's all right. I understand." It was clear that he did not understand. He looked disappointed as he ducked his head and moved off into the crowd.

I'm not over it.

Rebecca had said there would be flashbacks. It was another part of the healing process. She didn't say that the world would look different from now on. Different in a way that sent shivers down Ellie's spine. Or that ordinary people might give her the creeps when they said hello in the street.

It's temporary. It takes time.

She headed for the park to give herself some space. She felt suddenly fragile. And she couldn't remember feeling this way before.

It was relatively quiet in the park and there was something about the colour green, in all its shades, that was soothing. The wide footpath wound in and out of tall trees, around clumps of bushes, towards a pond where two children were feeding the ducks. Nice to be able to feed the ducks.

On the other side of the pond, sitting on a bench, was a young woman with auburn hair, wearing a black coat, leaning back with her hands in her pockets, looking out over the water.

Ellie sat down too, happy to watch the children. Today was supposed to be about a new start, but the bags at her feet suddenly looked ridiculous. Dinner with Dom would not change anything. Neither would his moving in. The healing process would take months, perhaps years. That's what Rebecca had said. And Ellie knew, despite everything, that she was on her own. It was up to her to banish the ghosts.

Bring it on!

But the challenge was just a little shaky.

The children's mother called to them to come away – she was talking to a man, laughing a little way off. The children emptied their bags onto the bank and ran to her. Ellie got up and went over to where they had been standing and picked up the bread that had not gone in the water. The ducks quacked their way towards her and she fed them. Life could be simple. It was just a matter of perspective. Then it hit her like a thunderbolt: How could she have been so stupid as to let Donna back into her life? She wasn't ready for any kind of contact. It had been idiotic.

When Ellie had received a friend request from Donna on Facebook, she'd decided for some crazy reason that she should do what she could to help her. It had felt just like when they'd been at school. Donna had wheedled her way in, somehow. Ellie had felt obliged to reply. How could she ignore such a heartfelt plea for help?

Dr Wilkinson, who knew of the request, had spoken with Ellie and said that she advised against it, insisting that it was far too soon and would cause unnecessary stress to both parties. Better to wait. Rebecca had been very concerned, too. So, the experts were in agreement: Ellie should not respond.

But, as always, she had made up her own mind. Stupid! And so, she and Donna had messaged each other. Donna wrote long, apologetic messages. She expressed gratitude for the generosity Ellie had shown in not prosecuting her. She had never meant any harm to come to anyone. She said that Joe and she were very close and that when she was better they would share the new flat. She missed him terribly. Donna was grateful for the help she was getting. Dr. Wilkinson was so kind. It was as though a huge weight had been lifted from her shoulders now that she was staying at the psychiatric centre and receiving therapy. When she was better, she would continue with her secretarial work. Dr. Wilkinson said that it would be good for her to take on a part-time job to start with so that she didn't feel stressed. Donna never mentioned Peter Benson.

Ellie had felt in control. It was harmless to chat on Facebook. But then Donna had asked to meet up, and she had said no. The messaging had stopped. It had been at that point that she had admitted to herself that what she felt was relief. She would let sleeping dogs lie. No more contact. Not for the foreseeable future, anyway. She'd told Donna her decision. Donna said she understood. Her last message had sounded sincere.

Walking back to the market, Ellie breathed deeply and regained the positive thoughts she'd had earlier. There was so much life around her. It was uplifting. The crowds were increasing, if anything. After-lunch-shopping. She looked at her watch – it was getting on for two o'clock and she was hungry and thirsty. Along three sides of the market square, there were shops and cafés. There was one particular café that sold nice cakes and where the service was friendly. She crossed the road and opened the large glazed door. It was warm inside and there was a delicious smell of freshly baked bread. Upstairs, she slipped off her coat and sat down. It would be nice to have someone to talk to, but Dom was teaching, and most of her friends were at work too.

"Hello, Ellie."

When Ellie looked up, she couldn't believe her eyes, let alone speak.

"I know. You didn't expect to see me, did you? But, here I am!"

"Donna?" The question came out like a whisper.

Donna didn't flinch. "Do you like my hair? I had

it cut and coloured. I saw you in the park. You looked so sad, Ellie. So I thought I'd come and cheer you up."

Donna slid onto the bench opposite, and the people in the café looked over at the brightly smiling girl, her chin resting on the palm of her hand, gazing at her friend.

"Thank you for everything, Ellie... I wasn't sure what would happen, you know? To me and Joe."

Ellie gaped. She still couldn't speak.

"I like it here," said Donna, breezily. "I like living in town. It's fun."

She found her tongue at last. "But, what are you doing...?" *What are you doing out of the hospital?*

Donna grimaced, as though she'd been struck. Then she smiled sweetly. "It's okay, Ellie. They let me out to visit Joe, three times a week. I have two hours. He's busy this afternoon, so I came to town for a walk. If you want me to go..."

The woman on the next table looked over. Ellie felt trapped. The last thing she wanted was to make a scene, here in the café. Very well, she would deal with it later. She'd call Rebecca. Speak to Dr. Wilkinson. For now, it would be better to humour her uninvited guest.

"No, it's all right. How... How are you, Donna?"

Donna smiled thinly and fiddled with her watch, then looked directly at her. "Oh, you know. I'm doing as I'm told."

Ellie tried not to think about the scar under the watch strap and how she had discovered it. What it had meant. She pushed back her chair. "Shall I get us a coffee and you can tell me about it, if you like?"

Donna nodded, her eyes too bright.

Ellie queued at the counter and ordered two

cappuccinos. It would be easy to leave. But that would be giving up, and she would not give up. She bought two muffins and carried everything back to the table on a tray. *On a tray*. She must place it on the table. *Don't slide the tray*.

"Are *you* all right, Ellie?"

"I'm fine."

"Only, you don't look so good."

"I'm fine, Donna."

"You're not worried, are you? You know, about Pete? That he might get to you? But now that, I mean… now that he's under lock and key… he can't get to you. Or me. Can he?"

It was difficult to believe what Donna was saying. *Under lock and key*. Was she seriously trying to intimidate her? There was that smile again. Just before she took a bite out of her muffin.

"Mmm! Great cake! I'm so glad I saw you in the park. Such a coincidence. This coffee's good too. Don't let yours go cold."

Any doubts Ellie had about Donna's state of mind disappeared. It was unbelievable. The girl was sick. There was no knowing what she was thinking. It would be better to go along with it, then leave.

The two girls were silent for a while. Ellie drank her coffee and ate her muffin, smiling at Donna from time to time.

I know what you're doing.

It was just like when they'd been at school and just like when they'd been in the cellar. Nothing had changed. Donna needed help. Help that Ellie could not, *would not*, give her.

When Donna broke the silence, she spoke a little

too loudly. "I don't blame you for any of it, Ellie. You've had a lot to deal with. It's no wonder you were confused."

Go along with it. She could have something planned.

Ellie nodded and said, "Not many people would understand how you could forgive me, Donna." It was easy to say things she didn't mean, when it meant coming out of this crazy situation safely.

"Thanks, Ellie." Donna put her head down, suddenly shy. "I appreciate your honesty. I really do."

"Don't mention it." Ellie hated herself for capitulating like this, but there was no other way. She saw now that Donna was capable of anything. Even in a public place.

There was a glint of metal in the sunshine. A knife lay diagonally across each of their plates.

Don't be so paranoid.

"All I ever wanted was to be your friend, Ellie. You have to believe me."

She had a sudden, ridiculous urge to put her hand over Donna's. The girl was a mess. She was on the edge of sanity. There were actual tears in her eyes.

Donna shook her head and snivelled, then tried to smile. "Sorry. Look at me! I should be happy! Everyone's been so kind."

The woman on the next table looked over with pleasant concern.

Donna stared only at Ellie and begged to be forgiven. "I've been a fool. I hope we can still be friends."

Ellie became aware that more than a couple of heads were turned their way.

"Yes. Of course we can."

The phone rang in her pocket.

"Leave it," said Donna, the light in her eyes suddenly extinguished.

Chapter Thirty-one

"Thank you for coming to see me, Joe. You did the right thing – it's getting to be a habit of yours." Alice Candy smiled. "With your help, we can make sure Donna doesn't get involved with the wrong kind of people. She needs to have the best chance of getting better. That's what we all want. If you go with PC Lancaster now, she'll drop you off near the meeting point. There'll be someone close by, keeping an eye on you, so don't worry. DC Brady and I will follow on shortly."

Joe had listened intently to what the inspector said. Without a word, he accompanied the officer along the corridor.

"He's a brave lad," said Alice Candy.

"Shall I call Dr. Wilkinson?" asked Will Brady.

"Yes. Tell her to get back to us immediately she knows where Donna is."

Alice Candy grabbed her keys and, moving more quickly than usual, made her way to the car pool, selected the first available vehicle and sat in the driver's seat. She put Ellie's number into her phone. It rang. There was no answer. The inspector closed her eyes and had a momentary vision of a pond, with children feeding ducks. Oddly, there was the aroma of coffee and freshly baked bread. The next image was more worrying, but it would not materialise – that meant it hadn't happened yet.

Will ran up and jumped in, just as Alice Candy

was putting the car into reverse.

"Do you think she'll do anything stupid, boss?"

"I don't know. But I'm beginning to think that Benson may have been telling the truth about Donna being the one who instigated the whole thing. There's more to this whole story, I'm afraid." She shifted gear and exited the parking area into traffic.

"Joe didn't corroborate his story." Will fastened his seat belt.

"No, that's true. But Joe *is* Donna's brother, and he's not as helpless as we've been led to believe. He's bound to be struggling with divided loyalties."

"He's a good guy, though?"

"Assuredly. It's not him I'm worried about."

They drove to the rendez-vous in silence, parked in a side street and waited.

"There's Joe." Will pointed to a figure walking across the footbridge to the opposite riverbank.

"Call Dr. Wilkinson again," said Inspector Candy. "I have a hunch that Donna has sent us on a wild goose chase."

*****

The day was pleasant, if cold. Joe walked along the riverside, past the entrance to the park, and scanned the benches. There were three. An old man sat on the first, reading a newspaper. The second was unoccupied. On the third, there was a young mother pushing a buggy back and forth. There was no woman wearing a yellow jacket. Joe scratched his head and checked his watch for the umpteenth time. It was still early. Five more minutes. He looked at the river, watching it flow past. His mother loved the river, and he wondered briefly how far away she was, knowing that she had flown half way round the world, but not being able to grasp the truth of such a distance.

For a moment, he missed her so that it hurt him in the middle of his chest. Donna had told him not to be upset when she had first left. *Mum will be back when she's seen her sister. If you were sick, you'd want me to be with you, wouldn't you, Joe? It's the same for Mum. Her sister needs her right now. We can spend more time together while she's away.*

But Donna had spent most of her time with Ellie and Pete. Then she had said that his mother was never coming back. Now, Donna was doing bad things again. Charlie was going to give him drugs for her. That's what Inspector Candy had told him. People like Charlie made a lot of ordinary people sick by supplying drugs that you couldn't get from a doctor.

Joe knew that Donna would be waiting when he got back. She would be angry with him for talking to Inspector Candy. But it was to save her that he had told Bella, and Bella had persuaded him to tell Dr. Wilkinson, who had told him he must go to the police. Dr. Wilkinson had said that Donna didn't know she was sick. That was the problem. She needed other people to help her get better, even though she thought she didn't.

He wanted to say, "Stop!" He wanted life to be simple. All his life so far had been to do with Donna and his mother. *Do this. Do that. That's good, Joe. Be careful, Joe. Remember what I told you, Joe. Don't trust anyone, Joe.*

Well, he would make his own decisions from now on. He would trust *himself.* Trust his own judgement.

The church clock struck two, and still there was no sign of Charlie. Then, he heard footsteps running up behind him.

"Joe. We have to go. It's urgent. Charlie's not coming."

Joe followed Will Brady, jogging as fast as he could. Inspector Candy was talking to someone on the phone as he got into the back seat and Will climbed into the front.

"Buckle up, Joe. We have to step on it." Inspector Candy spun the tyres as she pulled away.

Joe wasn't alarmed. He knew that he had put his faith in the right person.

Will Brady grinned at Joe, then glanced at Alice Candy's legs.

Chapter Thirty-two

Donna was getting more coffee. She was in no hurry to leave, it appeared.

Ellie had tentatively picked up her jacket and measured the escape route to the top of the stairs. Too risky. Donna didn't take her eyes off her for longer than a few seconds.

Then, she was back – sitting across the table, smiling as though this were all perfectly normal. Two friends enjoying each other's company. If only the other people in the café knew the whole story!

"Ellie?"

She was startled from her sombre musings. "Yes."

"Do you remember me?"

The question was odd. Very odd. "Yes. Of course I do."

"I mean, the *real* me. Amanda Leighton. That was my name back when we were friends at school. That's who I was."

Ellie swallowed hard. "I remember."

Donna wore a pained expression. She examined her hands, pulling on the fingers to crack her knuckles, one by one, before continuing: "You used to get out at the school gate and wave to your mother in the mornings. She always waited until you were inside, out of sight. Sometimes you didn't look back. But she still waited."

Ellie was uneasy. She didn't feel comfortable with the idea that Donna had spied on her. She pictured her mother clearly and couldn't hold back a small smile.

"That's the smile you gave her. Exactly like that!"

"Donna…" *This has to stop*.

"No. Let me speak, Ellie. I want you to know. I can talk to you. You'll understand. Dr. Wilkinson doesn't understand. She thinks she can make notes with her pathetic scratchy pencil while I talk. She thinks she can write a report to fix me. Whatever I tell her, she thinks it means something."

Ellie looked about her. She felt very conspicuous talking like this in such a public place. The woman at the next table got up to leave, sending over another sympathetic smile.

It was useless. There was no stopping Donna now. She seemed oblivious to everyone except Ellie.

Another memory came to the girl who used to be Amanda Leighton. "I saw you at the cinema, once. You were with your parents at the popcorn counter. Joe and I were waiting right behind you. You didn't see me…"

"I don't think this is helping…" She realised that Donna was talking about a time when they had been very young.

"Oh, but it *is* helping… You didn't see me, but I was there. If I'd wanted to, I could have reached out and touched you. But you know what? I was too scared. I just watched you. You were laughing. You had pink slides in your hair. You looked beautiful."

Ellie gazed out of the window at the crowded market square. She *had* seen Donna and her brother. She had seen they were behind her, from the corner of her eye. She'd held them apart from her, locked away in her peripheral vision. They were not the same as she was.

191

"Your friend, Lucy Statton, was there. You went over to say hello to her. You were talking about Caroline Bradshaw's party. She was going to be nine and she was having a big party at the weekend."

"Donna, you mustn't…"

"Mustn't what?" Donna's glare pierced Ellie with a shaft of pent up loathing. Her cheeks were very pink and her eyes as hard as ice.

Ellie looked at her watch, then towards the top of the stairs.

"You can't tell me what to do, Ellie. No one can. Not any more."

"I'm not, Donna. But I don't think it helps to drag up the past like this."

Donna took a sip of her coffee and set it down very carefully, as though it were a bomb that might just explode. Her gentle tone belied the look in her eyes.

"You're right, Ellie. I'm sorry. It's just that… well, it's been harder for me than for people like you."

Ellie shifted in her seat but didn't say anything. It wasn't her fault that Donna had had a difficult childhood, after all. Donna had too many skeletons in the cupboard. This was not the time or the place to bring them out into the light.

But Donna was insistent. "You are the only person I can talk to, Ellie. You know what it's like to be left on your own."

"Excuse me?"

"When your parents went away, when they left you – you know how it feels."

"I… Donna, they didn't *leave* me. They went to Spain to try something new. They…"

Donna reached for Ellie's hand. "It's all right, Ellie. I know how it feels."

She snatched her hand away. She bit her lip. She was furious. All of a sudden, she remembered the way she had felt about the girl who was always there, always hanging around, making everyone feel responsible for the fact that she had no friends of her own. Oblivious to the fact that everyone thought she was an incorrigible sneak and a crushing bore. Ellie was close to telling her, there and then. Letting it all come out.

But Donna hadn't finished. Her voice was edged with hatred now, her eyes narrowed in accusation: "You really shouldn't have been so arrogant, you know. At school. Always showing off. All your *pretty* clothes and *lovely* friends. It was truly a cheap way to score points, don't you think? The girl who wasn't cool, the girl who wore second-hand clothes, whose brother was *stupid* – oh, yes, I was an easy victim. Don't look so surprised, Ellie. Oh, you were better than most, it's true, but I knew you didn't really want to be with me. You were just trying to be nice to make yourself feel less guilty."

Ellie pushed back her chair. She didn't want to listen to any more. If she stayed, she couldn't trust herself not to tell Donna what would be best kept to herself.

Donna let out a small yelp. "No, Ellie. Listen. Don't be angry with me, please."

More heads turned.

Ellie leaned forward and spoke quietly but with conviction. "Donna, this is not doing you any good. I'm leaving. Don't make a scene."

Donna played to the crowd. "Don't go, Ellie. I need to talk to you. Just stay for a while longer."

This girl was hot and cold. Switching moods in an instant. Ellie shook her head, stood up and grabbed her bag.

"You should talk about this with Dr. Wilkinson, Donna." She spoke urgently but still discreetly, embarrassed at the worried looks they were getting.

Right on cue, Donna put her hands over her face and let out a sob. Another trick.

"I'm sorry, Donna. I have to go."

"Wait. Don't leave me here. I'll come with you." She stood up abruptly, rattling the cups on the table.

The girls were now the centre of attention.

For her part, Ellie knew that, one way or another, this was it. She was vaguely preoccupied with the thought that she and Donna would never see each other again just as soon as she could get out onto the street and call someone. But the present moment was bigger than such a thought. This moment was charged with dark expectation – Donna was unbalanced, and she would stop at nothing to make Ellie pay.

At the top of the stairs, impatient to get away, Ellie waited for a woman coming up, feeling Donna's presence behind her like an overbearing force. The stairs were steep, their edges cut sharp. She wanted to swing round and pull Donna. Take her by surprise. See her fall. But all she could take in was the strange elasticity of the moment – time didn't exactly stand still, but it moved forward in slow motion. A thousand flashed outcomes vied for her attention.

Then, Donna whispered something into her ear. "If this is the way you want it, Ellie. Just remember, you made me do this."

When Ellie looked around, Donna had gone.

Chapter Thirty-three

The house was closed up. No lights were showing.

"Would you like me to wait, love?"

"No. No, thank you. I have my key here. Goodnight. I'm fine. Really."

The taxi driver reversed into the yard then drove down the driveway, turning slowly out onto the road, looking back several times. He thought he'd noticed police tape, fluttering on the ground, but he couldn't be sure.

Sandra Barnes stepped over the threshold of her front door and put on the hallway light. The red tiles were stained with dried mud and in the kitchen there were dirty plates and a sideboard scattered with crumbs. Half a pot of coffee stood on the table. When she touched it, she tutted and shook her head. Stone cold. She put her coat on the hook behind the door and, leaving her suitcase for now, rolled up her sleeves and set to work to tidy the place up.

It was strange that neither Donna nor Joe was at home. But it was still relatively early, even though outside the darkness was as black as a tunnel. Perhaps they'd gone shopping and stayed out to eat. And, anyway, what could she expect? Here she was, coming home unannounced.

There was no point in trying Donna's phone again. She'd told her mother in no uncertain terms before she went that she wouldn't answer unless there was something urgent to tell her. And if there was, her mother should send a text. It would be cheaper. So that was what they'd agreed. Sandra Barnes sighed deeply. Donna was always so organised. But it had been very hard not to be able to talk to Joe. Very hard indeed.

The kitchen was tidy now, and the floors washed. The stove was lit and the kettle was coming to the boil. She put on the radio and sat down to a cup of tea and a sandwich. It was lucky that she'd called in at the Co-op to get a few supplies. There was nothing in the fridge and no bread in the bin.

As she ate, she began to wonder where her children could be. Perhaps they'd gone away for a few days. After all, the idea had been for Donna and Joe to spend some time together and for Joe to have some independence. She chuckled, remembering the huge grin he'd had on his face when she'd left. He'd been so excited about spending time with his sister that he'd forgotten to tell his mother he'd miss her! What fun they must have had without her. She certainly worried about Joe too much. He was ready to live his life on his own. Joe. She couldn't wait to see him, though. To put her arms around him. Her Joe.

Never mind. She'd see him soon, no doubt. Three months was a long time. Marian had told her to get back home in the end. She didn't have to stay any longer if it was making her miserable. *Stop moping about the place.* Marian had definitely seemed stronger. She would be able to cope without her sister fussing all the time. Sandra laughed to herself again. Marian certainly didn't like being told what to do! She stretched her arms above her head – thank goodness the operation had been a success! The doctors had been pleased. The prognosis was positive. There was really no reason for Sandra to delay coming home. What with Marian being so sure, the decision had been easy and now, here she was, sitting in her own kitchen, drinking tea from her favourite cup!

But where were Donna and Joe? Sandra was impatient to see them. She took out her phone for the umpteenth time. Oh, well. Maybe she'd send a text after all. She'd resisted so far, but now she must see them. Must see Joe. See how he'd changed. Donna would be the same, no doubt. She was a capable girl, if a little cold at times. Joe was the loving one.

An unexpected knock at the door almost made Sandra Barnes jump out of her skin. And when she opened up and saw a police officer standing there, it gave her an awful fright.

"What's wrong? What's happened? Oh, tell me nothing terrible's happened!"

"Mrs. Sandra Barnes?"

"Yes! Oh, yes. What is it!"

"Please don't distress yourself, madam. Everyone's fine. We received a call from a concerned taxi driver. There are some things you need to know about. Things that have happened while you've been away. May I step inside for a moment?"

Chapter Thirty-four

The traffic into town was not heavy, but drivers were unpredictable, slowing up to look for parking spaces, turning suddenly.

"Put the light on, Will. But not the siren."

It didn't make much difference.

"You okay, Joe?" Will looked over his shoulder.

"I'm okay," Joe answered. "You know where Donna is, don't you?"

Inspector Candy shot a look in her rear view mirror. Joe was a lot sharper than people gave him credit for.

"I don't think she's gone far."

"Are you going to arrest her?"

"I don't know. Let's not jump to conclusions, eh?"

People made way slowly. But there were no parking spaces. Alice Candy pulled up on one side of the square. She smelled coffee again and in her mind's eye she saw Donna and Ellie. She sensed imminent danger. There wasn't a moment to lose.

"Phone the fire station, Will. Send them round to the back of the building." She leaned into the car and whispered something in his ear.

Will Brady's eyebrows shot up, but he knew better than to ask questions. He just did as he was asked.

"Come with me, Joe," said the inspector. "I might need your help."

Alice Candy spoke quickly and clearly, as they

crossed the road. Joe listened carefully. She pushed open the door to the café and they went up to the first floor. There was a small group of people standing at an open door, discussing something with the manager, who stood undecided at the foot of the stairs, looking up.

Showing her badge, the inspector told the customers to go back to their tables and informed the manager that the police would handle the situation. Then, mounting the stairs, which led to the roof, she told Joe to follow.

In the distance, there was the sound of sirens approaching.

*****

Ellie swallowed hard and turned back. The café was hushed. A woman pointed to an open door on which there was a sign that said 'No Entry'.

There was a shabby landing and another flight of stairs. Ellie heard a door open at the top and felt a breeze coming down the stairwell, moving her hair across her face. Donna's words had been unspecific, but now they seemed ominous, and the blood drained from Ellie's face as she hurried up towards the fresh air.

She didn't know what to expect as she stepped out onto the roof of the building, but she imagined Donna standing on the edge, waiting to throw herself off. *Just remember, you made me do this.*

The sky seemed close and the noise from the street distinct. She could hear traffic and conversation, the occasional clatter of metal, or the sound of a horn. Beneath her feet, the roof was flat and covered in fine, white grit with sparse, strangled weeds growing here and there. Donna was nowhere to be seen. Not until she turned around.

Sitting with her legs hanging over the side of the low parapet, Donna stared straight at the ground below, hitting the side of her head with her hand rhythmically. When she spoke, she repeated the same word over and over again, "No, no, no." The way she said it was not in anger or desperation, but more as though she were telling off a small child. "No, no, no." Again, she hit herself, this time slapping her face with first one hand and then the other.

"Donna?" Ellie approached warily.

"Too late. Too late, Ellie. You had your chance."

"This is a bad idea, you know?"

Donna gave her a contemptuous look and shuffled closer towards the edge.

"Wait!" Ellie came nearer and sat down as close as she dared.

The ground seemed a long way down. There was still the sound of sirens in the distance. But this did nothing to reassure her. How could they be anything to do with her present situation?

"Oh, Ellie!" Donna lunged for Ellie and wrapped her arms around her, outstretched, sobbing into her lap.

"Be careful, Donna. We'll both fall!"

Donna looked up, still holding fast. Again, her mood changed. There was ice in her eyes and a grotesque grin spread over her face. With one huge effort, she pulled Ellie towards the edge and tipped her off balance so that, had it not been for a narrow ledge and a precarious grip on the hard, dry brickwork, she would have fallen.

She let out a scream just as Alice Candy and Joe emerged through the door.

"Donna!" It was Joe. He came running, ignoring the inspector's warning to stay back.

Ellie felt herself slipping. One arm now flailed in empty space. The other clung determinedly to the wall. She tried to get another handhold in an effort to stabilise herself, but she was too low. She heard voices from the roof and voices below. Her feet were too big for the ledge, which gave little purchase, her single hand grip would not hold much longer. And all she could see was Donna's awful face – the girl was smiling, waving goodbye with one hand as a child would, watching Ellie's fingers slide. Joe was coming, she knew, but he would be a second too late. In one last effort, and with no thought for the consequences of her action, she grabbed Donna's leg and pulled hard, lifting herself enough to find Joe's strong hand, as he thrust it over the top, crouching low to keep his balance. At the same time, Ellie was aware that the grip she had taken on Donna's leg had been solid for no more than a moment, and she took in the jerk of Donna's body, glimpsing the shock on her face as she fell. Joe did not loosen his grip, despite his sister's scream.

He laid Ellie gently on the ground and held her hand.

"Thank you, Joe. But…"

"It's all right, Ellie. Don't worry," he said.

Alice Candy stood over the two of them and glanced down to where two firemen were helping Donna out of the jump net.

Will Brady was there, looking up at her. Had she imagined it, or had he winked? Of course she had imagined it. Of course she had. But hadn't she noticed the same thing once before? The incongruity of this thought left her surprised and momentarily distracted.

Stooping to talk to Ellie, she gave Joe the warmest of smiles. "Donna is fine. If you don't believe me, ask Joe."

"The firemen caught her in their net. She's okay. I promise."

Ellie sat up.

"How are you feeling?" asked the inspector. "Can you walk?"

All around, people began to unfreeze. The people in the café, the people on the street, the fire crew and the people who had flocked to watch the rescue. Everyone began to breathe again. No one had been hurt. Ellie would be fine and Donna would be taken into custody. This time, Ellie would have to say what really happened. Happy endings. *Do you believe in happy endings, Alice?*

Joe went down to his sister, who was being looked after by a paramedic.

"It's okay, Donna. I've got you," Joe murmured.

He held his sister close and listened to the sounds of her letting go. It was the first time he had heard Donna cry.

"What have you done? What have you done, Joe?" she sobbed.

This time, there was no need to answer. It was over. Donna knew it. And Joe knew it, too.

"Can I go with my sister to the hospital?" he asked.

"Of course you can," replied the paramedic.

When Dom arrived to take Ellie home, Will Brady

met him outside the café. Inside, Ellie was being spoiled and comforted. Alice Candy stood by, inscrutable, her expression somehow luminous. "Donna's all right, Mr. Bryant. Just give her a moment."

Dom wanted explanations. "How did Donna get to her? We thought she was locked up."

"Not exactly. Under supervision. Not the same thing." Will put his notebook away. Stuck his pencil behind one ear.

Dom looked inside the café but couldn't see Ellie.

"She's out back. There's a staff area. They're making tea, I think." Will took out his phone. "We're going to need a statement from her, I'm afraid."

Dom nodded. "Can I go and see her?"

"Of course." Will pushed the door open and indicated a door at the back of the shop. "She's just inside."

Turning to Alice Candy, he asked, "How did you know we'd need a net?"

"Instinct," she grinned.

"The fire chief said they were lucky to find one at the station. They became obsolete about twenty years ago, but then I'm sure you knew that too."

The twinkle in his eyes made her feel giddy. "If that's what you think, Will Brady, then who am I to tell you otherwise."

Chapter Thirty-five

Alice Candy was exhausted. She opened up her office and held the door for Will before going to her desk and collapsing into the leather swivel chair. The case had turned out to have more twists and turns than a fairground ride.

"How did you know where Donna would be?" Will asked, lowering himself into an armchair by the window. "And how exactly did you know we would need the fire service?"

"I didn't know for sure." Alice Candy didn't tell Will about the smell of coffee, the park or the ducks. She didn't say that she had sensed that someone would fall from a great height. "But I did know that Ellie was planning to go into town. When Donna went AWOL, I suppose I just put two and two together. When we got to the square, it was just – "

"Gut feeling? Telepathy? Alien intervention?" Will smiled broadly.

Alice smiled back. "Don't ask, Will. You know I don't understand it, myself."

Will nodded. He knew how it was.

After a pause, the inspector added, "And there was the red herring, of course. Joe came to us, remember? With the story about Charlie. *Charlie*! Donna couldn't resist her little joke. She knew that Joe wouldn't get it."

Will raised an eyebrow. "Even so, Charlie being synonymous with cocaine is still not much of a clue to the meeting Donna had set up."

"No. No, that was incidental, but crucial in the long run. You see, Donna *expected* Joe to go to the police. It was part of her plan. Get Joe to lead us on a wild goose chase. There we would be, waiting by the river on the other side of the park, for a girl wearing a yellow jacket, leaving Donna free to corner Ellie in town and get her own back."

"So, Donna knew where Ellie would be?"

"Yes. They were friends on Facebook, remember. It only remained for her to get into town and find Ellie in or around the market square. The hospital had Donna logged out for a visit to Joe's. She hadn't put a foot wrong in weeks. No one would suspect anything. Simple."

"But, how did Donna know that Ellie would go to *that* café?"

"She didn't. Ellie told us that it had probably been Donna who was in the park, sitting across the pond from her. It's just that Ellie didn't recognise her. Donna was biding her time. The café was a bonus. It meant she could get close to Ellie in a public place and let her know that she was not forgiven. That she owed Donna, somehow. The door to the roof presented itself and Donna saw an opportunity."

Will whistled. "You are really something else, Alice Candy!"

There was a comfortable silence in the room for a moment, hung with something more intimate. An unspoken empathy.

Then, leaning forward, Will asked, "Do you think she planned to *kill* Ellie?"

"I don't know. I don't think we ever will. One thing is sure, though. This time, there's no scapegoat. Donna will be charged with assault at the very least and the charge will stick, if I have anything to do with it."

A telephone rang in the outside office, then cut off.

Will glanced back to his boss. She looked peaceful with her eyes half closed. He mused aloud. "Benson's appealing for a re-trial."

"He'll get one."

There was no need for explanation.

"There's one person I feel sorry for," Will continued.

"Who's that?"

"Joe. He's a good lad."

"No need to feel sorry for Joe. He's decided to stay on in the flat with Jess. His mother has moved back into the family home – now there's a woman who had a lucky escape."

This last comment awoke Will's interest once more.

Alice Candy had opened her eyes and was looking straight at him. Will Brady looked adorable. "Don't you see? She would have been Donna's next victim."

Alice Candy picked up a pencil from her desk and spun it round and round in her fingers. "The plan was to get rid of her all together. My guess is by fire. Burn down the house, with Sandra Barnes inside, probably drugged first. Then Donna would be able to claim on the house insurance. Mrs. Barnes said that before she went off to Australia, Donna had insisted on her making an appointment to bring her life and house insurance up to date. Mrs. Barnes thought it reasonable under the circumstances, with a long journey coming up. Donna stood to be the primary beneficiary, bearing in mind Joe's learning difficulties."

Will let out a long whistle. "You are amazing.

You know that? I wish I had a mind half as sharp."

Alice Candy allowed herself a smile. "You're not so bad, yourself, Will Brady. Now, get off home before I insist you take me to the pub for a double gin and tonic!"

Will grinned and took his cue, strolling easily back to his desk before slipping on his coat. Alice Candy let out a wistful sigh. It had been a long time since she'd been taken out for a drink by an attractive man. A very long time indeed.

She locked her desk, turned out the light and secured the office door. When she reached the bottom of the stairs and walked out into the night air, it was difficult not to throw her arms wide and whoop for joy.

"The King's Head serves a good gammon and chips." Will stepped out from the shadow of the building.

Alice acted casual, kicking a pebble into the gutter. She looked askance at the very handsome young man who knew that she would accept his invitation.

"I'm partial to gammon. Nice with a slice of pineapple and a dab of mustard." She took Will Brady's proffered arm, her long slender fingers white against the cloth of his coat.

"English or French?"

"English, of course!"

*****

The next day, there was a knock on her office door. Sandra Barnes was standing on the other side of it, looking as though she were about to be hung, drawn and quartered. If there was anyone Alice Candy felt sorry for, it was this woman. Just then, Joe arrived too with a barely controlled Jess in his arms. The inspector got up to let them in.

"This is an unexpected surprise!" She stroked Jess and closed the door, inviting her guests to sit. "What can I do for you?"

"Inspector Candy, we have to know what's going to happen to Donna." Mrs. Barnes folded and refolded the scarf she had removed from her neck.

Joe smiled and put an arm around his mother's shoulder. "She'll be all right, Mum. She'll be all right, won't she, Inspector Candy?"

The guilelessness of the young man's enquiry was almost unbearable, and Alice Candy wondered whether she would be able to say anything that might be comforting and at the same time true.

"She's committed a serious crime, Joe. Isn't that right, Inspector? If Joe hadn't caught that girl…" Mrs. Barnes spoke slowly, her words laden with quiet grief.

"There's no need to speak to me like a child, Mum. I know that Donna's done a bad thing. But she's sick. She needs help to get better, and that's what she'll get, won't she, Inspector?"

Alice Candy gave him a straight answer. It was what she was sure he wanted. "It's not quite as simple as that, Joe. Donna will need to be re-assessed before she goes to trial."

"How long will she get, Inspector?" Mrs. Barnes was close to tears.

"I really can't say, I'm afraid. It's nothing to do with us, now. But you can be sure that Donna will be treated fairly."

Joe wanted to say something more. "What is it, Joe?" asked the inspector.

"Donna didn't treat Ellie fairly. She locked her

away and wouldn't let her out. She told me that Ellie was her friend and she wasn't at all. She lied to me. Then, if I hadn't been there to catch her, Donna would have let her fall."

"Joe, what are you saying?" Sandra Barnes was clearly emotional.

"The truth, Mum. Sometimes the truth is hard to take. But, we still have to say it." He stroked his mother's back and kissed the side of her head.

Inspector Candy smiled.

"Well," said Mrs. Barnes, making an effort to pull herself together. "You seem to have it all straight, Joe."

"I have, Mum. Thank you for seeing us, Inspector. I'll take Mum and Jess home now. I've got sausages for dinner tonight." He looked shyly over at Alice, before adding, "Would you like to join us?"

His mother looked panic stricken. "Don't be silly, Joe. The inspector's busy. She doesn't want to waste time – "

"Yes, Joe. If that's a serious invitation, I'd love to. Sausages are one of my favourite things!"

When Joe and his mother had left, Alice Candy picked up the phone and spoke to her daughter.

"Would it be all right to pop over at the weekend?"

"Mum! Really? You're not working?"

"No, I'm not."

"Then, yes! Come for lunch."

Alice Candy slipped on her coat and locked up her office. The weight of the last few weeks was beginning to lift. Of course there would be more to do, but Will would cope with most of the paperwork. What mattered now was that she was going home for a hot bath, after which she would spend a pleasant evening in the company of one of the nicest people she'd ever met. On the way home, she bought chocolates and some doggy treats. Life could be simple, sometimes. She looked in the hall mirror as she hung up her coat, and smiled.

"Welcome home, Alice."

Made in the USA
Columbia, SC
25 February 2023